The war th

The Viet Cong ███████████████████ ally.
They could ble█████████████████████tack
by surprise.

Just like Mack B███ ███ doing now.

He flared into action. Tran Le was directly behind
him. Bolan and the girl took back-to-back positions
and went to work.

Bolan scored a double-head hit. The frontal assault
of two guards became a backward slide into hell.

Tran Le's Type 56 stuttered steadily. The big guy
sprinted to the doorway and crashed through, his
AKM up and ready.

He gave the place a quick once-over.

No prisoner!

The wall shackles dangled empty where Bolan had
seen the captured American only two hours earlier.

Colonel McFee was gone.

Bolan's gut turned cold with rage and anticipation.

Now he was left to his own devices.

Now, at last, was the kind of Vietnam war he could
win.

About the author

The story of Don Pendleton's rise to success reads much like the fiction he has created. A native of Arkansas, Pendleton left home at 14 to join the navy. "I didn't falsify any documents, I simply told the recruiters I was 18 and they signed me up." He saw action in World War II in the North Atlantic, North Africa, Iwo Jima and Okinawa, and, later, in Korea. After the War, he completed his high-school equivalency and worked as a railroad telegrapher, air-traffic controller and as an executive in the aerospace industry.

Married and the father of six, Pendleton describes himself as a self-taught writer, "simply a storyteller, an entertainer who hopes to enthrall with visions of the reader's own innate greatness."

The exploits of his hero, Mack Bolan, have sold 30 million copies in North America, 65 million worldwide. The Executioner series has been translated into 12 languages and is sold in 125 countries.

MACK BOLAN

THE EXECUTIONER 43

BOLAN

Return to Vietnam

DON PENDLETON

A GOLD EAGLE BOOK FROM

WORLDWIDE

TORONTO · NEW YORK · LOS ANGELES · LONDON

First edition July 1982

ISBN 0-373-61043-2

Special thanks and acknowledgment to
Stephen Mertz for his contributions to this work.

It is true to say that the glory of man
is his capacity for damnation.
The worst that can be said of most,
is that they are not man enough
to be damned.
                                    —*T. S. Eliot*

Man is that part of reality
in which and through which
the cosmic process has become conscious
and has begun to comprehend itself.
                                    —*Julian Huxley*

Don't ask me about right and wrong,
good and evil. All I see is a blind
dumb universe that sees only when I see,
hears only when I hear, and weeps
only when I weep—and I know only
what I can and cannot accept.
I cannot accept hell on Earth.
                          —*John Phoenix (Mack Bolan)*
                                    from his journal

Dedicated with pride to all who went,
with compassion for those who did not return,
and with understanding for those who did.
Historians of a less fragmented time will
accord the rightful honors ... for whatever
comfort that may be.
As for our MIAs—God forgive us all.

U.S. Prisoners in Vietnam: Although the Defense Intelligence Agency proposed in 1979 that the private sector sponsor any investigation into POWs in Southeast Asia, it was the CIA that launched a secret probe to Attapey in 1981. The operation was the result of aerial reconnaissance that showed 30 non-Asians at hard labor in an area of Laos known to be honeycombed with caves. That mission was unsuccessful, but Meo tribesmen have continued to claim the existence of U.S. prisoners in Laos and Vietnam. The Vietnamese government is bankrupt and, say observers, they could be keeping the Americans to bargain for money, food and medicine. Now that ex-Special Forces officer Bo Gritz's *Operation Eagle* rescue venture has been scotched by the DIA because of "the political undertow," it is missions like Mack Bolan's that currently hold out the best hope for the luckless POWs in Vietnam.

The Montagnards: Mountain warriors from the central highlands of Vietnam. At one time a highly religious agricultural people, they have recently become known for their fierce rebellious activities in the Army for the Restoration of National Independence.

The Meos: A tribe of Montagnards, more formally called Hmong, whose individual groups are distinguished by the costumes of the women (White Meo, Blue Meo, Red Meo, Flowered Meo, etc.). There are 150,000 Meos in Vietnam. Bolan once lived with the Meos for six months during the Vietnam War.

PROLOGUE

Every war is immoral. Bolan knew that. In the everyday contest in which life flowers, nothing is more destructive to the human ethic and to the human spirit than the savageries of warfare. War is immoral. It is a widowmaker, an orphanmaker, a babykiller; it is death and misery let loose in wholesale lots, hell unchained, devolution.

Immoral, yes, always... in the near look. But, then, man had always been at war with the shadows of hell. At war with hunger, with disease, with the planet itself. And he had learned early that he must forever be at war with himself.

Heaven does not come by simple proclamation. This had been Bolan's illumination as a young warrior. Every heaven is earned in hell. It is earned, usually, in warfare of one type or another. In that sense, then, no war is ever truly immoral, not in the long look. It was, indeed, perhaps the single most ennobling pursuit ever undertaken by humankind, the most distinguishing characteristic of the species. Unlike the other forms of life, man did not adapt to the unacceptable. He changed it, by God, and in the process changed himself, evolving as a result of conflict instead of becoming a pliant reed through which the evolutionary force would flow blindly—the only life on Earth that shaped its own destiny.

This was Bolan's illumination, yes. And it had built a formidable warrior, a truly tough man who could command the spirit to labor in hell with heaven in view. Which is to say that he did not struggle blindly. To lose sight of the paradox, to allow the long view to totally eclipse the near reality of hell itself, was to become something less than human. A true man—the noble warrior—did not wallow with a sense of glory in the slime pits of mankind's war upon itself. He detested it, deplored it, wept over it— yet all the while continuing the struggle, determined to wrest from chaos something noble and enduring, something positive and constructive for humankind; even though in his secret heart of hearts he knew that he would not recognize the prize if he should encounter it.

No...he would not recognize the prize. He would see nothing but wailing widows, stunned orphans, brutalized men and maimed babies, death and destruction, madness and misery. He would see hell itself. But he would most surely plant his feet and try to build a heaven there, never quite certain within himself what heaven is or should be.

Yes, this was Mack Bolan's illumination. He had found it in Vietnam, here in this unlikely outpost of hell, and he had carried the light as best he could through the darkest jungles. As a result, some in this land had come to call him *The Executioner*. Others had called him *Sergeant Mercy*. But he had always known he was neither. He was simply a warrior, fighting hell. Later, through one of those unacceptable events that shape man's reactions to his environment, Mack Bolan discovered that Southeast Asia is not the only, nor even the worst, outpost of hell. He found one in his own little corner of heaven—or of what he had perceived as some form of heaven—*home*—and the illumination flared into a blinding light, which would dim only in death. Bolan became, truly, the Executioner—the conscious tool of a cosmic process that had begun before the shaping of any heaven or any hell, before any concepts of good and evil, of morality and immorality.

Immoral, yeah. The first ''immoral'' war had been fought here. Bolan did not believe that for a moment, except in the sense that all wars are immoral in the near view. The most hideous immorality of that particular war, in Mack Bolan's long view, would be found with those who had not fought it, who had pressed and clamored for a loss by default, demanded ignoble retreat from hell's front doorstep, then had compounded the infamy by dishonoring the returning warriors and robbing them forever of the simple spiritual dignity that any man earns in challenging hell. Worse—far worse—was the persistent suspicion that some had even been abandoned and forgotten to languish forever, building neither a heaven nor a hell for themselves or anyone else, sacrifices in purgatory by a people gone too soft to challenge hell for real.

That, in Bolan's long view, was hell realized... and the greatest immorality of all. He would not accept it. He was a civilized man in an evolving species and he could not accept it. He was, by God, going to change it...if he could. He was going back to Vietnam.

1

The AV-8B Advanced Harrier, the Marine Corps' latest VTOL (Vertical Takeoff and Landing) jet craft, skimmed the treetops near Haiphong, North Vietnam, in the 3:30 A.M. darkness, traveling at a speed of 600 mph, holding low enough to avoid detection by radar.

The plane had been modified to accommodate one passenger: a big man in battle black who had come from halfway around the world to this point in time and space; from the peaceful environs of the well-camouflaged Stony Man Farm command post in Virginia's Blue Ridge Mountains to this final countdown into a high-priority mission.

The man was Mack Bolan, now known as Colonel John Phoenix.

And the mission was a return to Vietnam. To these same hellgrounds that had first spawned the Executioner.

Mack Bolan's "journey" here had begun long before his hurried departure from Stony Man Farm a mere twenty hours earlier. In fact, his unofficial title, the Executioner, dated back far earlier in the Bolan history than those Mafia-busting days of the seventies, when a young penetration master from the ranks of the U.S. Army's Special Forces had returned stateside to declare and wage a magnificent, morally motivated war of his own.

The mob had not been obliterated. But they had been slowed down—the result of being hit where it counted often enough by the Bolan Effect—to where now a renewed, geared-up Justice Department assault on organized crime was able to contain their activities to such mob "fringe industries" as legalized gambling and prostitution.

And Bolan's attention was needed elsewhere.

A New War had been declared, this time with "Colonel John Phoenix" fully sanctioned and backed by the White House.

It was an open war against the dark, destructive side of Animal Man, wherever, however, and in whatever form he reared his ugly head.

Jack Grimaldi was piloting the Harrier. They were some 350 miles inside the Socialist Republic of Vietnam, zipping along in a northeasterly direction at a near-suicidal altitude of fifty feet above the blue green jungle.

Bolan was outfitted for night combat. The powerful .44 AutoMag pistol, Big Thunder, was slung in its holster, suspended over his right hip from a military web belt. The silenced Beretta Brigadier 9mm pistol was leathered beneath his left armpit. Extra clips for both pistols were stashed in canvas pockets clipped to the military belt that circled his waist. An AKM assault rifle with the stock folded was slung over his shoulder, as was a waterproof pouch that contained assorted hard punch incendiary and fragmentation grenades, plastic explosives, and a variety of light penetration gear.

He rode in an ejection seat, with the parachute on his back making it a damn tight squeeze.

Grimaldi's voice crackled through Bolan's headset.

"Hold on, Striker. I'll be taking her up in another thirty seconds or less. It's going to happen fast."

"I'm ready, Jack. Thanks for the lift in."

"No big deal. I just wanted along for the ride."

Bolan knew better, but he let it pass. The time for conversation was over.

During this final brief hiatus before the action began, Bolan's thoughts touched one last time on his "new war" and on the urgent mission at hand. They were inextricably entwined.

Thoughts of the Vietnam War intruded. A time that most Americans would probably rather forget, and with good reason.

But it was a time when brave men had taken a life-and-death stand over ideals and concepts that mattered a lot to Mack Bolan.

True, there had been politicians and profiteers, both Vietnamese and American, who had exploited the conflict to meet their own selfish, unholy ends. But their venality in no way negated the basic issue that had been fought over these Far Eastern lands, that had taken so many allied and American lives.

The issue had been, quite simply, aggressor versus victim.

Human dignity and freedom versus tyranny.

Yeah. Damn straight. Bolan and his buddies *had* fought the Good Fight down there, despite as much flak eventually from the home front as from the Cong.

Then it had ended, and America's fighting men were called home, the fight taken from them for a while, and the enemy, Cannibal Man, had advanced a few more hundred miles across the world map, devouring the weak and defenseless every step of the way.

But it should have been over as far as America's involvement was concerned.

Yeah.

Should have been.

Except that the Vietnam conflict, and all it embodied, was reaching out its smoky tendrils from the past to ensnare Mack Bolan in the here and now.

Bolan had long been aware that many servicemen remained unaccounted for from the Vietnam War, and that most individual cases had already been reviewed administratively by our government, resulting in a PFD (Presumptive Finding of Death).

Yet during the past couple of years there had been approximately one thousand reports—including three hundred firsthand sightings—of American prisoners of war still being detained inside Vietnam.

Until a very short time ago, all such reports had remained unconfirmed in government agency files. The situation had remained at a frustrating deadlock and, it appeared, would remain so indefinitely.

In 1981, the Vietnamese government released the bodies of thirty American service personnel who formerly had been listed as MIA, claiming that they had no further information regarding any Americans. There were, the Viets said, absolutely no American POWs presently in Vietnam.

Yet the reports continued.

A Swedish journalist came back with news of having seen American prisoners shackled hand and foot and forced to work alongside a Viet rail siding. *"Tell the world we're here! Tell them not to forget us!"* is what the Swede heard.

Refugees, too, came out with stories of having seen American prisoners.

The thought of it pulled Bolan's gut even tighter now with an anger that was both hot and cold.

Cold because Bolan never lost the icy, cutting, objective edge that was the essential ingredient in a professional combat soldier—the edge needed to stay alive in the world he inhabited. If he ever lost that edge, he was dead.

But it was a hot anger, too, when Bolan considered the immense, incredible sacrifice of those men left behind.

Unlike the other 2.7 million returned vets, unlike

all Americans, they had not been free to move into the future, to absorb the good and the bad, the best and the worst of the Vietnam experience into their psyche and their lives, and move on to other—hopefully better—things.

Not these poor mothers' sons. Uh-uh. They were still mired in the muck of that rotten war.

They were probably Special Forces people, mostly. Men with information that could mean a lot to the enemy. Some were imprisoned in forced-labor camps simply as brutal revenge.

Bolan had been aware of the situation, and he had reacted with bitter disappointment when the 1981 U.S. commando raid into Laos in search of American POWs had turned up nothing.

No, there would be no shortage of hot spots in Bolan's new war. The world was his theater, and he moved across the stage of this epic drama that was his life, taking the priorities as they were handed to him by Hal Brognola, Stony Man's liaison with the White House, or as his own conscience dictated.

But there had been no handle for Bolan to grasp regarding the Vietnam POW problem.

Until now.

Until Brognola had shown up at Stony Man Farm twenty-one short hours ago with information that could make all the difference to a large number of Americans still held prisoner in this far-off corner of the world.

On this mission Bolan was going in to pull out only

one man, but that man held the key to where many, many other Americans were being held all across Vietnam.

The mission would be among Bolan's toughest. The man he hoped to rescue was interred in a maximum security prison for which Bolan and Grimaldi had only approximate coordinates.

If Bolan's intel was correct.

And the clincher was that Bolan *knew the guy*.

There were far too many ifs involved in this mission for Bolan's liking. But of one thing there could be no doubt—Mack Bolan was willing to put everything he had, everything he was, totally on the line to get that man out, no matter what the odds.

And on this mission, the odds could not possibly have been higher.

But the big man in black was ready.

And willing.

And—bet on it—*very* able.

2

Grimaldi's voice sounded again through Bolan's headset.

"All right, Striker. Get ready to strike! Here we go."

Bolan nestled himself back as securely as possible into the Harrier's ejection seat. No more time for conversation now. No more time for anything.

It was happening.

Grimaldi worked the controls, and the jet pulled into an abrupt ninety-degree climb with barely a fractional slack in speed.

Bolan began counting.

His reality became a near-deafening high keening whistle, with the sensation that his vital organs had been left down below. His head snapped back from the force of the jet's climb.

He counted to zero, then punched the ejection button. There was a blast of sound and he was slammed like a kicked football into the blackness of night.

Another count.

He released the chute.

It billowed outward and snapped him upright,

breaking his fall at six hundred feet with a *pufff* sound like some amplified human voice expelling air.

Over his right shoulder he saw that Grimaldi had already put a good distance between them. The Harrier had gone into a smooth dive and was moving away from Bolan, again beneath the radar grid.

The plane had probably shown up for ten seconds or less on any monitoring radar screens, if it had been noticed at all. And if the blip was noticed, Bolan was deliberately being dropped some seventeen miles away from his objective so that the drop would not be immediately associated with his mission.

Grimaldi punched the Harrier's afterburners and got the hell out of there. With a thunderous scarlet orange *whoooooooosh* that lit up the nighttime sky, the Harrier was suddenly and completely gone.

A gently falling Bolan felt his lips tug into a grimace of respect for Jack Grimaldi. Bolan himself was a fine pilot, yet he would be hard pressed even to approach Grimaldi's expertise.

Silently he wished Grimaldi godspeed back to the pilot's destination, a covert U.S. commando base and airstrip somewhere in the north of Thailand near the Laotian border.

The flight had been the last step of the jump-off into this mission. Grimaldi would be returning to the base, his phase of the mission completed—for now.

Grimaldi had plenty of reason to get out in a hurry, before he had company from the Viet air force, before SAMs started filling the air.

The American powers-that-be had considered long and hard the political ramifications of utilizing the USMC craft in penetrating Vietnamese airspace. Indeed, the VTOL was devoid of all identifying markings. But in Bolan's opinion those powers need not have worried. Not with Grimaldi at the controls. Their hardware was safe in the very best of hands.

As he swayed downward, Mack Bolan scanned the black void that seemed to yawn beneath him like deep space.

Then he saw it.

A small fire, one kilometer to the south. Grimaldi could not have been more on target.

Bolan tugged the chute cords, steering his descent toward the prearranged rendezvous below.

When he was still some seventy feet above the tree line, a silvery half-moon shone through the low cloud cover overhead, illuminating the geography he was dropping into at the same time that the smell of the jungle rose up to smack him in the face like some tangible thing.

Yeah.

Nam.

The jungle.

The stink of decay—animal, vegetation, human—enveloped him in the humid darkness. He could make out the lush treetops of jungle growth; they seemed to billow out like nightmare clouds, making the darkness beneath him even deeper.

The geography undulated in transition between the

mountainous region to the southwest and the flat plains of the Red River Delta to the southeast.

Cutting a winding, quarter-mile-wide swath through the jungle plain was the dark flat ribbon of the Sông Hong (Red River), several kilometers off to Bolan's right; it was one of the major tributaries feeding into the delta.

As he came down, Bolan triggered the flashlight unit attached to his hip, sending the prearranged signal of three long beams in the direction of the fire.

Then he relaxed his body for the jarring impact of landing, which was only moments away.

There was a major military installation in the region where the Sông Hong emptied into the delta. The base was a principal railhead that was used for transporting arms and munitions south across the highlands during the war. Although the importance and activity of the base had diminished considerably, it was still utilized by government forces as a routing station for supplies, including weaponry, from Haiphong to points west and north.

On the outer perimeter of the base, but within its patrolled boundaries, stood—*if* Bolan's intel was correct—an ancient temple constructed during the Han Dynasty (circa 100 B.C.).

At present, however, the temple was far more than the innocent ancient edifice that had been vacated and declared off limits to local civilians because of military activity during the war.

According to Hal Brognola's briefing just prior to

Bolan's departure from Stony Man Farm, the "temple" had been converted and fortified by the Viets into a maximum-security military prison.

And there, according to the intel, was where Mack Bolan would find Colonel Robert McFee.

The Executioner remembered Bob McFee well from the Sniper Team Able days of Bolan's military career. McFee had been MI liaison with the CIA on several of Bolan's missions into the North. Bolan remembered liking and admiring McFee as a good, tough soldier and as a fine, compassionate human being who had shared Bolan's dedication to the work they were involved in.

After the war, McFee had been numbered among those American service personnel—usually men like McFee with Vietnamese marital ties—who had willingly stayed behind after the American withdrawal, men who were now involved with the various political underground groups in guerrilla actions against the ruling Vietnamese government.

Bob McFee had spent the last decade living and fighting with a Meo tribe of Montagnards, the fierce mountain warriors who comprised the group known as the Army for the Restoration of National Independence.

The Meos themselves had passed this information along to the U.S. government one day earlier, via the American Embassy in Bangkok. The Meos also relayed the news that McFee had been captured by the Viet military, and the fact that they knew where he was being held.

But the prison was maximum security, and the guerrilla group was requesting the assistance of a military penetration specialist to aid in breaking McFee out.

The Meo rebels had reasons of their own for wanting McFee sprung, of course. The American had served the Meos in an advisory capacity long enough to learn the entire network of underground groups functioning in Vietnam. The Meo fighters could not afford to have that information slip into the hands of the Viet authorities. It was vital to their lives and their cause that they rescue McFee before he was forced to divulge this information.

But the Meos had passed along one final tidbit to insure America's interest: on his own, during his travels throughout Vietnam, Bob McFee had been gathering information concerning the exact whereabouts of close to three hundred American service personnel being held prisoner by the Vietnamese government...

It was the hottest tip that this country had yet received regarding the U.S. POWs.

It was the handle the Executioner had been looking for.

The jungle reached up to grab Mack Bolan in its smothering embrace. The parachute caught in the treetops and broke his fall with a body-wrenching jolt. His feet swayed six feet from the jungle floor.

It had rained sometime during the past half-hour. Everything was wet in this jungle world. The steady *drip-drip-drip* all around him, and his own breathing, were the only sounds he heard. His arrival had temporarily silenced the insects and other night sounds.

He released himself from the chute straps. He fell to the ground, landing in a tight crouch.

The AKM swung around and out into firing position, fanning the stygian night around him.

The Executioner had landed.

He was truly home.

Back in the element that had borne him.

On a life-and-death mission that meant everything in the world to this American fighting man.

Bolan moved warily toward the signal fire some four hundred yards away.

From this distance, he could vaguely make out the form of a lone Meo, waiting for him in the faint and flickering light.

The mission had begun, yeah.

The game of death was in play.

3

The diesel-powered sampan carrying Bolan and the two Meo tribesmen cut through the glass-smooth waters of the Sông Hong.

The terrain along this stretch of river was almost primeval—unchanged since the dawn of time. Dense jungle grew down to the lip of the riverbank.

The damp closeness of lush plant life made the muggy night air even more oppressive.

The only sound was the eternal symphony of jungle night life all around them—bats, birds, monkeys, insects—underscored by the muted putter of the sampan's engine.

Three times during the past thirty minutes the flat-bottomed skiff had passed through heavy swarms of mosquitoes, and each man had tossed his own net over himself for protection.

At the moment, Bolan's net was heaped beside him on the deck. He rode just forward of the sampan's mast. The AKM lay beside him to his right. His finger was wrapped around the trigger.

He wore a round-brimmed straw hat tipped forward on his head, as if he were a Vietnamese who had drifted off in a light sleep.

The semblance of a breeze had come up. The mosquitoes had disappeared, for which Bolan was damn thankful.

Despite the humid night air, a cold chill had touched the base of his spine. Some sixth sense was warning him. He *sensed* danger....

It was 0410 hours.

Thirty minutes since Grimaldi had dropped him in.

Bolan still wore his blacksuit and full combat rigging. Upon close inspection he would fool no one as a Vietnamese. But he didn't expect anyone to get that close.

The two Meo tribesmen who had come for him were squat, barrel-chested primitive men outfitted for this occasion in standard Vietnamese loose-fitting black pajamas. Each man was armed with a ChiCom issue Type 56 automatic rifle—most likely captured from NVA units during the war—which was essentially the same weapon as Bolan's AKM except that the Type 56s were manufactured in China.

Though small of stature, these fierce mountain fighters carried themselves proudly erect. Pride also shone from their eyes. They and those like them were the survivors of their race. The last warriors.

Mack Bolan's kind of men.

The kind he could trust.

Subdued greetings had been exchanged in Vietnamese. Then the three men had made their way from the small clearing to the banks of the Sông Hong back-river tributary a short distance away, where the sampan was waiting. Another ten minutes, and they had rejoined the Sông Hong itself, moving downriver in a southeasterly direction into the outer reaches of the Red River Delta lowlands.

Right now they were still another forty minutes away from the temporary Meo base for this operation, which was a small cove two miles upriver from the temple-prison.

The past twenty minutes had passed in silence between Bolan and the two Meos. They were a people of few words.

The journey thus far had been uneventful, for which Bolan was again thankful. These outer reaches of the delta were sparsely populated and only lightly patrolled by government troops.

The sampan chugged past an occasional sleepy village of thatched huts, past dark-green patches of fields partially hidden behind bamboo clusters and trees, past wider expanses of rice paddies that were irrigated with networks of dams and sluices whose design dated back thousands of years.

But the jungle was never far away.

And the jungle instinct in Bolan's gut told him that the mission could not be as effortless as all this. Not by a damn sight. He knew with a certainty that the longer they traveled without opposition, the closer they were to their first confrontation with that opposition.

He tossed a glance at the Meos.

Both tribesmen were sitting back by the engine. Their high-cheekboned faces were impassive. They appeared supremely confident and deadly.

Bolan reflected on what he knew of the Meo tribe of Laos and North Vietnam. A primitive tribe of mountain people? Maybe. But they embodied characteristics, ideals, and philosophies that earned them a place of honor and respect in Bolan's mind.

The Meo had first migrated into Nam from China in the early nineteenth century. They were farmers, mostly. They cleared away and cultivated their own small agricultural communities from the burgeoning vegetation that was always threatening to encroach and reclaim what had been carved from it.

Life was a constant fight for the Meo. A constant struggle against adversity from both natural and human elements.

But the Meo had met the challenge head-on. The tribe had been involved in a long series of rebellions against the racist, authoritarian ruling governments of Vietnam, dating back to 1862.

In Vietnam there were still deeply rooted prejudices against the Meo, who are properly called Hmong, which were aggravated most recently when the mountain tribe worked extensively with American Special Forces units in Laos during the war.

Bolan had once lived for six months in a Meo village in the Laotian highlands, on a CIA mission for which Bob McFee had been his control in those combat years so long ago, the years when Bolan had worn a double sobriquet, "the Executioner" for the superb work he did, and "Sergeant Mercy" after those humanitarian instincts and practices that made him a walking legend among GIs, Viets, and Montagnards alike in this war-torn land.

As a result of their alliance with the Americans, the Meo had found themselves the victims of a government-directed campaign of mass genocide and were all but wiped out by vengeful Communist troops in the years immediately following America's withdrawal. All that now remained of the once powerful tribe were scattered pockets of proud guerrilla fighters like the group who had made contact with the embassy in Bangkok.

Fighting for their survival had schooled these "primitives" in the most modern of combat techniques and weaponry. They were the remnants of a people dedicated to fighting for their own simple way of life—and to finding always a way to hang on and fight back.

Yeah, these men had Bolan's admiration, and no mistake.

Noble savages?

Uh-uh.

Make that noble *warriors*.

Bolan snapped his attention out of his reverie and back into the moment at hand. And at that very moment, their luck ran out.

The jungle night noises around them ceased abruptly, totally.

The two Meos caught the vibes, too. One of the tribesmen flicked off the diesel engine. No words were needed. For a few seconds, stillness reigned.

Then Bolan's ears picked up the distant throaty hum of a larger engine advancing toward them from the inky darkness downriver. It sounded less than one klick away, approaching at a steady rate of speed.

The river curved sharply three hundred yards ahead. The approaching craft was not visible, but Bolan could see a reflection in the water at the bend that was cast by what must have been a high-powered searchlight, far stronger than anything needed for simple river travel at night.

This stretch of river may have been lightly patrolled, as the Meos thought. But Bolan and company were about to come eyeball to eyeball with one of those patrols unless they moved fast.

Bolan whispered over his shoulder in curt Vietnamese to the men steering the sampan.

"Pull us over to the bank. Everyone get down."

The Meo at the helm obeyed with alacrity. The sampan curved silently through the murky water. Within moments the skiff bumped gently against the riverbank.

Bolan glanced around, hoping to find some overhanging vines or foliage for the sampan to hide behind. But the tree line began another several hundred yards away at this point. Elephant grass grew down to the lip of the bank.

From the reflection in the waters up ahead, it appeared that the patrol boat's spotlight was rotating from bank to bank of the river in wide, lazy sweeps. Bolan knew the only chance out of this problem without tipping their hand was if the army boat's spotlight happened to be on the opposite bank as it passed, missing the sampan. A confrontation at this point would only imperil the ultimate objective of rescuing McFee and getting him to safety.

Bolan reached into his pouch and extracted the infrared Starlight spotting scope. He focused in on the bend in the river as the patrol boat chugged into sight.

The craft was exactly as Bolan had expected. A shallow thirty-five-foot diesel-powered launch, unarmored but well armed.

The five-man crew of the patrol boat lounged about its deck in attitudes of relaxation. Bolan could make out their weapons clearly in the scope's greenish glow. Each man was armed with a Kalashnikov AK-47 assault rifle, another weapon essentially the same as Bolan's except that the AK-47 was slightly heavier. One RPD machine gun was mounted at the boat's bow; another was mounted atop the low cabin that extended four feet over the stern.

Bolan registered two more facts in a flash of ascending battle consciousness.

One was that the patrol boat's spotlight would indeed be hitting the sampan if it continued its normal rotating course.

Bolan and the Meos were crouched low. The barrels of three automatic rifles rested across the rim of the sampan, following the course of the patrol boat.

The second fact was that the one approaching army boat was not alone. . . .

Bolan swung the Starlight scope upriver. Until now the noise of the second patrol boat's engine had blended in with the first. This boat was designed and equipped to match the other, right down to number of men and types of weapons.

Patrol Boat Number Two was now at 150 yards and closing fast with a powerful rotating spotlight of its own.

Fate could not have dealt Bolan a worse hand to play.

Incredibly, the two boats would rendezvous or pass each other at a point abreast of Bolan's sampan.

The Executioner swung into action before that could occur.

It was not this man's style to sit by and wait for his fate to come knocking. The Bolan philosophy called for shaping and guiding one's destiny to the best of one's ability.

That is what he did now.

Mack Bolan commenced battle. He announced his presence there on the Sông Hong with full-force hellfire and fury.

And the killing began.

4

Bolan snapped a whispered command at the Meos.

"The boat on the left—*take 'em!*"

Then he focused his attention on the army boat closing in from their right. His finger caressed the AKM's trigger.

The weapon began blasting and bucking in his grip, lighting up the pitch-darkness with silver strobe flashes, spitting a blistering, tightly patterned dozen rounds that took out the spotlight on that approaching boat even before it swung around to take in the sampan.

Shouts and frenzied activity from both boats.

The Meos opened fire with their Type 56s. The other patrol boat's spotlight disintegrated. The battle zone was thrown into total darkness again except for muzzle flashes.

A machine gun opened up from the boat on the right. But it was aimed too low. Slugs made angry *plip* sounds in the water a few yards short of the sampan.

Bolan set his AKM down close beside him and again reached into his pouch, this time withdrawing one of the M34 incendiary frag grenades.

He yanked the pin with his teeth and heaved the missile at Patrol Boat Number One.

The M34 carried only a four- to five-second fuse. It hit the deck of that patrol boat with no time for any of the hapless soldiers on board to reach the thing and toss it away.

The grenade exploded the night wide open—and several bodies along with it, lighting up the blackness ten times brighter than the rifles had. The boat lifted momentarily from the water, wreathed in a flaring sheet of death.

Screaming bodies pitched through the air. The clap of the explosion swallowed up the machine-gun fire. Then Bolan heard loud splashing sounds as the airborne corpses and parts of corpses plunged into the water only short yards from him.

Bolan swung the AKM back into action. An angry exchange of automatic-weapons fire was clattering between the Meos and the other boat. Shouts of pain and confusion and the splashing of more bodies sounded from that direction. The Meos were holding their own, so Bolan continued to concentrate on the boat he had zapped with the grenade.

He kept the AKM on automatic mode and swept the deck of the crippled boat with a wide figure-eight pattern, sending in a blitzing hail of 7.62 tumblers on a withering search-and-destroy of anything that had survived the grenade blast.

Bolan heard a *slap* sound and a loud expulsion of breath nearby from within his sampan. He held his fire and looked just in time to see one of the Meos tumble over the side of the craft under the power of a direct hit. The body sank from sight.

The surviving Meo was crouched low in the skiff, returning steady fire at Patrol Boat Number Two.

Only one of the RPDs and two AK-47s were firing from that boat. The Meos' fire up until now must have been taking its toll. But the rounds from the enemy boat were snapping into the side of the sampan and whistling into the night all around Bolan.

The firing from Boat Number One had ceased entirely. Bolan again shifted the AKM and reached into his pouch.

The remaining Meo fed another clip into his rifle. The big American, holding his finger steady on the trigger to keep the Viets on that boat temporarily pinned down, pulled another M34 from the pouch, tugged the pin, and lobbed this grenade as accurately as the first.

Another direct hit.

The near-blinding explosion took out not only the three Viets but the patrol boat's cabin as well, hurling chunks of debris and corpses into the air.

There was no more firing from either boat. Only silence.

"Let's move!" Bolan instructed the Meo.

The single tribesman grunted assent.

The sampan's engine coughed to life. The skiff glided away from the riverbank, catching the river current again.

The current also carried what was left of one army boat into the other. Bolan scanned the decks as the sampan moved past. He could see the wrecks littered with the dark forms of torn bodies. Nothing moved.

But he kept the AKM up and ready, just in case.

Within moments the Meo had steered the sampan away from the patrol boats, and they were on their way again.

Behind them, the army boats drifted idly, receding into the darkness.

Another half-kilometer and the nighttime jungle noises resumed as if nothing had happened.

Bolan relaxed a little. He looked at the surviving Meo.

The Montagnard's expression was impassive as ever. Except for his eyes, which were violently alert.

"I'm sorry about your friend," Bolan told the man.

"It was quick," replied the tribesman in a monotone. "He is out of this now. We still have another nine kilometers to go. But this is poppy country. When the army finds what has happened back there, they will think it was done by smugglers. There is often such fighting along this route."

"You are a brave man, my friend," said Bolan. "What is your name?"

"I am Krah Dac."

Bolan extended a hand.

"Krah Dac, you have my respect and admiration. As do your people."

The two men shook hands briefly. The Meo's grip was firm and strong.

"We are more than friends, American," said the tribesman. "We have spilled blood together in battle. For that, we are brothers."

Bolan could not have put it better himself.

The Meo were, yeah, his kind of people.

Good men to fight with. And good men to die with, if it came to that.

The big American and the mountain warrior lapsed back into a mutual silence. They understood each other. There was nothing more to say.

The sampan glided on through the early-morning darkness. It was 0425 hours.

Bolan considered the consequences of the delay they had just suffered. It was essential that he make a soft probe of the temple-prison downriver before the all-out assault to spring McFee, and it was nearly as essential that such a probe be made under cover of darkness. Which meant that time was rapidly running out, since the sunrise was probably little more than an hour away.

Despite its intensity, the encounter with the patrol boats had been brief. But before he could get to the prison, Bolan still had to make contact with the Meos at their temporary base camp situated in the cove ahead. If they really pushed it, though, there might still be time.

Not that Mack Bolan would consider aborting this mission under *any* circumstances. It was, yeah, worth the Good Fight all over again in Vietnam. To Mack Bolan, it was a mission worth dying for.

The next two hours would be life-or-death time in the Red River Delta, for sure.

5

When Bolan first saw the eerie pink glow reflected from up ahead by the low cloud ceiling, he estimated that their sampan was no more than one and a half kilometers away from the scheduled rendezvous with the Meos at their temporary base camp.

Krah Dac stood up in the rear of the skiff, without taking his hand from the rudder.

"A fire," said the tribesman. An expressionless statement of fact.

Bolan pegged the source of the flames to be about one and a half kilometers downriver. He felt a sinking feeling in his gut.

"Can you kick any more knots out of this thing?" he asked the Montagnard.

"The engine is old," replied Krah Dac. "It does the best it can."

Bolan experienced a strong sense of déjà vu as the sampan carried them closer to the source of that fire reflected overhead. He had seen this land at war. He had seen similiar skies reflect similar fires many times during that war.

He realized that for the Meo sharing the sampan

with him, it would be far more than déjà vu. For Krah Dac and his people, it had become a way of life.

And death.

This lush jungle nation of 126,436 square miles, inhabited by over 45 million people, had been plagued by the curse of war and civil violence since long before Christian times. It was a land of sudden death where life was very cheap. Bolan wondered if it would ever change.

The armies of Vietnam defeated Kublai Khan in 1288. They were, in turn, conquered by the French in 1859. During World War II Vietnam was occupied by the Japanese, and atrocities were committed everywhere. In 1945 the troops of Ho Chi Minh came out of the hills and overthrew the regime sponsored by Japan. The French tried to reclaim Vietnam in a bloody war that ended in the slaughter at Dienbienphu in 1954. Within another decade, it was America's turn to fight in these jungle hellgrounds. And Bolan knew that the violence and killing had not slackened a bit since America's pullout. Death and more death, all of it over a rural countryside whose only claim to fame was its moderate export of rice, rubber, and coal. Yet outside forces would not let it be. Vietnam had never known peace. And the end was nowhere in sight.

Another kilometer and the sampan would reach the cove from which that fire was almost certainly reflected.

Bolan tossed another glance at the Meo. He could

see that Krah Dac's eyes were staring at the wavering glow overhead. The shimmering pink color was mirrored in the Montagnard's marblelike eyes.

Uh-huh, thought Bolan. *The guy knows what we're going to find when we reach that cove....*

The impression was confirmed a moment later when the tribesman spoke.

"Will it never end?" he asked, as if addressing those reflected flames. For the first time a note of anguish, which he must have felt to the pit of his soul, crept into Krah Dac's hard monotone. "Why can they not let us be? Why must there always be the killing...?"

Bolan had no answer.

The fires had all but died out by the time Bolan and the Meo tribesman cautiously approached the scene on foot. They had grounded the sampan and split up.

Once they had ascertained that the area was free of any military presence, both men emerged from opposite sides of the clearing that bordered the small cove where the Meo guerrilla group had been encamped.

The area was free of life altogether.

Bolan felt his face harden into a grimace as he surveyed the scene of devastation that stretched before him.

The Meos must have arrived after dark and not gone into the jungle, which was their first mistake. They might have figured that they'd be on the move again before dawn, so lack of lights had probably been their only camouflage. Two sampans and three slightly larger boats were grouped together, bobbing gently just offshore.

There was charred, dismantled debris everywhere—weapons; equipment; barely recognizable, smoldering human remains. The jungle tree line thirty yards away had been scorched and blackened.

The stench of roasted flesh hung heavy in the air.

There was no "universal brotherhood of love" here in this bleak cove on the Sông Hong. No philosophical blather. There were only slaughtered victims of aggression. There was only death and the smell of the dead everywhere.

It took Mack Bolan right back to those early days of an earlier war.

Bolan counted nine bodies. Some of the corpses had escaped the flames that had devoured the boats. Several bodies were sprawled across the clearing in near-impossible positions, bent out of shape by the powerful rounds fired from the air, which had ripped the life forces from them.

Mack Bolan turned away and lit a cigarette.

One anguished teardrop etched its way down his cheek. But he was damned if he would wipe it away.

It was a tear of anger, of frustration, of having looked over the edge one more time into that dark pit of what humans are capable of doing to each other.

It was a tear for mankind.

Krah Dac crossed the clearing toward Bolan. The Meo took a long look at each body on the ground as he passed it.

When he reached Bolan, the American saw that the Meo's expression was still impassive, still impossible to read.

"It looks like an air attack," said Bolan. "There aren't any signs of ground fighting. Helicopters with napalm and machine guns from the army base by the prison. There was no place to run."

"This, as well as the patrol boats on the river... they must know of our plans," said the Meo.

Bolan grunted. "It's possible. Or it could just be lousy luck. I've been on missions that were jinxed. Everything went wrong. It can happen. But what about your group leader? He was to meet us here. Did you see his body?"

The Montagnard shook his head. Then he nodded in the direction of the floating ruins that had been their boats.

"Perhaps he is among those. Many bodies are terribly burned. I recognized only a few. One was my brother."

"I'm sorry, Krah Dac."

The Meo waved Bolan's words away. "It is done and cannot be undone."

"It can be avenged," said Bolan. "When did you arrive at this place?"

"Last night. One boat at a time over many hours.

Then the other man and myself went to meet you. Now...this.''

"Could one among your number be an informer?"

The Meo drew himself erect.

"Never! We are not mercenary fighters, Colonel Phoenix. We are fighting for survival. We do not inform on ourselves. It would be taking our own lives.''

In the silence that ensued, Mack Bolan heard faintly the sounds of people moving in toward the clearing from two separate directions in the nighttime jungle.

Krah Dac heard it too.

Both men fell to a combat crouch, swinging their weapons up to port arms. Bolan fanned the darkness off to their right with his AKM. Krah Dac did the same to their left with his Type 56.

Now what the hell?

The insect sounds were stilled once again. Bolan strained to listen. It sounded like four people approaching, two people from each direction. Still, it took the keenest of hearing to detect the sounds. Whoever was coming this way, they were either pros or simply in their natural element. Or both. But they were not the untrained sounds of civilians who might live in the area, coming to investigate what must have been one noisy massacre while it lasted.

At that moment Bolan was ready for anything to come his way out of the jungle.

It had been that kind of mission since he had landed. Thus far not one element had run according to plan. There had been nothing but violence and slaughter and the worst possible twists of fate.

Mack Bolan was a realist.

He knew damn well there was every reason to expect more of the same.

Very soon.

6

The rustle of approaching movement through the jungle undergrowth ceased.

A bird call cried out from the darkness. In the stillness of the jungle at that moment, the new sound carried with striking clarity.

From behind him, Mack Bolan heard Krah Dac relax slightly. Bolan looked over his shoulder at the Meo.

The tribesman had slung his auto-rifle over his shoulder by the strap. Krah Dac raised his hands to cup his mouth. He emitted a bird call that rang in the gloom with crystal purity, identical to the first.

Another answering call came back from out there, slightly different from the first two.

Then those out in the darkness continued to close in.

Bolan also relaxed, but only slightly. His finger never left the trigger of his AKM. And he never stopped scanning the inky darkness with unblinking eyes.

"Friends of yours?"

Krah Dac grunted. "It appears not all of our group

was caught here tonight. It is Sioung Tham, our leader."

The cloud cover parted before the moon overhead once again, just as four people emerged from the scorched jungle tree line.

The moonlight in the clearing gave everyone a chance to eyeball each other as the four new arrivals walked up to Bolan and Krah Dac.

Bolan saw that the four approaching him were also Meos. Three men and one woman, all armed with Type 56 auto-rifles that matched Krah Dac's, and dressed in camouflage suits. All four wore their hair long and moved with catlike grace.

When they reached Bolan and Krah Dac, one man—obviously the leader—stepped forward toward Bolan with his hand outstretched.

"You are Colonel Phoenix?"

They shook hands. The Meo headman was somewhat older than the others, but his grip packed the strength of a man half his age and twice his size. The Mont's primitive face was lined and scarred. Part of his right ear was missing.

Bolan had not known until this moment that this was the tribal leader he was to work with. He knew this man! On that mission those lifetimes ago when Bolan had lived and worked for six months among the Meos, the man had once journeyed from a distant village to pinpoint a secret NVA base for Bolan, where one of the Executioner's targets had been lying low.

Lifetimes ago, yeah.

John Phoenix had been Mack Bolan in those days. Another man with another face, before his fierce War against the Mafia had altered his name and life, and before plastic surgery had altered his features.

Bolan and this man had spent little more than a day together that one time. But yeah, Bolan remembered the warrior.

As for the Mont, he had no reason to link that time and that Executioner with the American agent standing before him in the darkness now.

"I am Phoenix," Bolan grunted. He felt a moment of inner frustration. But the past was gone. Bolan/ Phoenix lived in the *present*, and too many bridges to that past had already been burned for him to consider breaching the extreme care, security, and sweat that had gone into creating his new persona and this new war. So be it. "Sioung—you are named for the nineteenth-century warrior chief of your people. A man famous for his strength and heroic deeds," affirmed Bolan.

The Meo headman stepped back from the greeting. His eyes were impossible to read. He surveyed the carnage around them.

"There was no heroism here tonight. Only sacrifice."

The woman of the group walked up to the leader. She placed a hand on Sioung's arm.

"I am sure there was much heroism here tonight, father. And do you forget the helicopter that we brought down only two kilometers away?"

Sioung shook his head slowly.

"That will not bring back those who died here," he said with great sadness.

Bolan gave the woman a closer look in the clear moonlight. She seemed to be about twenty-six or -seven, but she had the fresh complexion of a Meo girl ten years younger. Her camouflage suit did not conceal the pert rise of her breasts nor the sleek lines of her hips and thighs. Her high-cheekboned face was highlighted by the warm almond eyes and sensual mouth that denoted the singular beauty of women of this part of the world.

She was a looker, yeah. A lovely flower amid the horror and death in this inlet. But Bolan had a hunch that she could be as deadly as she was beautiful, too.

Bolan returned his attention to the headman.

"Were you out there watching Krah Dac and me for very long?"

Sioung nodded.

"We thought you may have been followed from upriver. We waited until we were sure you were alone."

"How could this massacre have happened?" Bolan asked.

"My daughter, these men, and myself went to observe the temple where our mutual friend is held," replied Sioung. "We go for one hour. As we return, we hear sounds of attack in this direction. Army helicopters passed over us after killing is done. We open fire. We lose one man. But we bring one chopper down. Then escape and come here."

"Krah Dac and I also ran into trouble upriver," said Bolan. "We lost another of your men. Do you think the army knows there will be an attempt to rescue McFee?"

"We have much misfortune on this mission, but that is all. There are always patrols. Boat and helicopter. And when they find Meos, then often times Meo die. But if army knew of plan, then choppers would not have returned to base. This cove would still be watched. And there would be more than two army boats on river. It is only that the gods frown upon us, for reasons I do not know."

One of the Meo men who had been with Sioung stepped to the headman's side. He glared at Bolan with angry intensity as he spat words like bullets.

"Sioung, I respectfully disagree. You know why the gods are angry as well as I. This American from across the water brings us bad luck."

"McFee is an American," replied Sioung, just as sharply. "McFee has helped us. Fought with us. We must help him."

"And watch more of our brothers and sisters die?" demanded the angry one. "We are far from our home in the mountains. McFee worked with us, yes. But do we owe him so many lives of our people? Let this American, Phoenix, rescue McFee if that is what he wishes." In one sudden fluid motion, the warrior swung his auto-rifle around from his shoulder so that it was not aimed at anyone but was grasped at port arms in an attitude of supreme competence. "We are Meo!" he announced. "We must avenge what has happened here tonight. But in our own way. On our own ground."

Bolan met those burning brown eyes with his own steady frosted blues.

"You are a Meo, and so I know fear is unknown to you," he said to the man. "And I know that what happened here in this cove tonight is happening to your people all over Laos and Vietnam. You don't want to lose any more people. But you will lose many more, my friend, if the men who have Bob McFee force him to talk. I understand that he knows the details of the organization you call the Army for the Restoration of National Independence. Many more of your people than those here tonight will die all over this country unless we get McFee out in time. And to do that, we must work together."

The dark-haired lovely who was the headman's daughter nodded her agreement.

"The American is right, Deo Roi. Your grief clouds your vision. We must be strong together."

Bolan appraised the young woman with a new sense of admiration. She was beautiful, yes. And yeah, she looked as if she knew everything there was to know about the heavy Type 56 assault rifle slung over her slim shoulder.

But she had brains, too, and a fair way of looking at things with a cool head. She was the kind of woman who always appealed to Mack Bolan: highly competent but with the inner spark of her femininity intact.

Deo Roi looked from Bolan to the woman and back again, catching what must have been in Bolan's eyes. The young buck started to snarl something else.

But Sioung lifted a hand, and the words were still-born in Deo Roi's throat.

"You will argue among yourselves no more," the headman bristled. "I have heard enough. There is much to do and little time. Deo Roi, you will hold your tongue and obey your chief. It is your duty to this unit and to our cause. You are one of the best Meo warriors, and so I will forget the words you have spoken in anguish." He nodded to the woman at his side and at Bolan. "But both Tran Le and Colonel Phoenix speak the truth. I asked the Americans to send us a man. Colonel Phoenix is that man. Sioung does not go back on bargains he has struck. We will return to the temple now, before dawn, and we will work *together*. Do you understand, Deo Roi?"

The young buck did not return the headman's angry stare. "It shall be as you command, Sioung."

Deo Roi spun away from the confrontation. He stepped between Bolan and the headman's daughter as he stalked off to stand beside Krah Dac and the other warrior several feet away.

Bolan did not fail to notice the searing glower of dislike that Deo Roi fired in his direction as the Meo lapsed into silence. Bolan knew that he had made an enemy by the very fact of his being here in this place at this time. And yet there seemed to be something considerably more behind Deo Roi's dislike for him.

Bolan snapped his attention back to Sioung. He also glanced at his watch. It was 0450 hours.

"Time is running out," he agreed with Sioung. "I want to slip into that prison myself before the attack to see it up close. I suggest we move out immediately."

Tran Le replied before her father.

"You cannot enter the prison alone, Colonel Phoenix. That would be suicide. The temple is on the perimeter of an army base. It is heavily guarded."

Sioung nodded agreement.

"I think it best if we attack in force, Colonel. A quick, hard strike. We take the prisoner and—"

Bolan interrupted Sioung with a shake of his head.

"A brave plan, Sioung," he said. "But Deo Roi's point is a good one concerning our loss of manpower because of what has happened in this cove. We cannot afford to risk any more lives. The best way is to know exactly where to hit that temple and with how much firepower. The only way we'll be able to determine that is for one of us to get inside and try to find exactly where they're holding McFee. I am the penetration specialist you asked for. I believe I am the man for the job."

"You are truly so, Colonel," Sioung said quietly. There was deep respect in his voice.

Bolan was pleased he had won the Meo's respect. But he had neither time nor inclination to hear his own praises sung.

"How long will it take us to reach the temple?"

"A twenty-minute hike through the jungle, if we hurry."

"Then let's go," grunted Bolan. "It's time I got a look at this prison."

The group started off into the jungle without another word and without a backward glance at the horror they were leaving behind in that cove.

Bolan knew that the numbers on this mission were falling away rapidly now. Not just the number of personnel he had expected to back him up—Sioung's guerrilla unit had been chopped to less than half its size. But time also was slipping away.

It would soon be dawn.

A new day.

In a new war.

But Mack Bolan, the Executioner in combat black, was prepared for whatever that day might bring.

Victory.

Death.

Or both.

7

Mack Bolan and the five Meo guerrillas walked two abreast along the jungle trail, which was little more than a path running a half-kilometer in from and parallel to the Sông Hong.

Another hundred kilometers downriver, and a traveler would be surrounded by the industrial-metropolitan complex of Hanoi, the busy urban hub of North Vietnam.

But Bolan was now in the farthest outlying reaches of the Red River Delta. There was much more jungle here than population or cultivation.

At many points along the dark trail, tangled growth reached down to slow their way. Along other stretches, their route skirted marshland and swamp with only occasional expanses of rice paddies. There was no inhabitation along here. They met no one. Traces of a wispy morning fog made clear visibility come and go.

The eastern sky was etched with the first faint traces of dull gray. But Bolan judged the actual sunrise to be another twenty-five minutes away. On the ground it was still night.

The big American strode along, trying to ignore the impatience building in his gut. But they should reach the riverbank opposite the temple within ten minutes or so. The action would begin soon enough.

Sioung and Deo Roi had taken the lead. Then came Krah Dac and the other warrior, whose name was Y Bo, followed by Bolan, who marched alongside the headman's daughter, Tran Le.

Bolan was thinking again about Bob McFee and some of the times—the best and the worst—that they had shared when McFee had been Bolan's CIA control in the long ago. Bolan had only actually socialized with McFee once. It had been at a tiny outpost just short of the DMZ when the colonel and the young penetration specialist sergeant had been waiting alone in a room for final orders for Bolan's Able Team, while the orders had somehow been tied up at headquarters.

There had been time to kill, and Bolan and McFee had drifted into shooting the shit the way two men will—not as officer and noncom. Bolan remembered several such instances during his tour in that strange war, but only this one time with McFee. Men had needed moments of *humanness* over there, free of rank and any of the realities around them, in order to keep their sanity. It had been such a moment for Colonel McFee.

The two men had spent the evening swapping memories about their backgrounds and what they hoped to go back to when the war was over. For no reason at all, Bolan found himself recalling that McFee had said he'd like to get into the hardware business when he got back home. . . .

Bolan's focus shifted to the present when he noticed Deo Roi up ahead. The angry young warrior had glared over his shoulder briefly at Bolan and the headman's daughter.

It was the third time since they had begun the trek that Deo Roi had done this.

Bolan pitched his voice in a low whisper and spoke to the lovely Tran Le.

"Deo Roi dislikes me," he said. "And I think there's more to it than our words back at the cove."

Tran Le's smile flashed in the darkness.

"You are a perceptive man, Colonel."

"Are you and Deo Roi lovers?"

"Ah. You are also a direct man. Both qualities to be admired, I think."

"You're not going to divulge any information you don't want to, are you?"

She studied him for a long moment in the darkness before responding.

"Deo Roi would like to be my lover," she said at last, speaking low. "He would like to be my husband. I have considered this, and I do not think it could ever be. As you have witnessed, Deo Roi is impulsive and at times irrational. These are qualities that I do not admire in a man."

"Why does your father keep him on?"

"Because Deo Roi is also a strong, brave warrior.

He is a Meo, and his dedication to our cause is beyond question.''

"And what of you, Tran Le?" asked Bolan as they maintained their pace. "You have the strength and beauty of a Meo woman, and yet there is something different about you. You speak English very well."

"I was lucky, Colonel Phoenix. There are benefits to being the daughter of a tribal chief. I was schooled until my seventeenth year by the missionaries who once lived among us. I was always...different, somehow. I would look over the mountains of my home and rather than feel protected and safe, the way I was supposed to, I would wonder what was on the other side."

"Perhaps someday you will travel beyond this land," said Bolan, and turned to look at her.

"Perhaps. But everything changed once the government began its genocide of the Meo. Now my place is here, fighting with my people. Not somewhere else, reading about it."

"Tran Le, you are perceptive also. And a very special woman."

Sioung lifted his hand at the head of the small procession. They halted some ten yards short of the point where the trail widened and the jungle fell back.

Bolan reached over and gave Tran Le a warm squeeze of the arm.

Then he left her side to join Sioung and Deo Roi.

"River is just ahead," Sioung told him. "This fog

protect you. But you must hurry. The fog will lift soon.''

''Where are we from the prison?''

''Across from it. A short distance across the river. Come, I show you.'' The tribal headman looked at the others. ''Stay here for now,'' he instructed them. ''Be alert. There may be patrols.''

Then Bolan and Sioung moved ahead. They broke from the jungle tree line. The land sloped down slightly for another ten yards, to the bank of the river.

The morning fog was a swirling mist that was already beginning to dissipate within the first five feet or so of the water level.

Bolan and Sioung stretched out flat at the lip of the bank. Bolan pulled the Starlight from his pouch and focused in across the river. They were lying at an angle that permitted Bolan to see beneath the heavier fog, through the swirling mist, toward their objective.

The Sông Hong looked to be a quarter-mile wide at this point. They were at a slight downriver angle from it. The river was untraveled at this early hour. The water was calm, smooth.

The eastern sky behind the temple was taking on its first pinkish tinge. The temple was silhouetted for the Executioner's inspection.

Sioung spoke softly at Bolan's side.

''Gaze upon history,'' is all he said.

The prison that held Bob McFee was well camouflaged. Although some details of the edifice seemed hazy to Bolan because of the slight mist and the greenish glow of the spotting scope, he could still see that the structure resembled only what it appeared to be.

Bolan was looking through the Starlight at a work of ancient art that rivaled the greatest man-made objects anywhere.

The temple was composed of one principal three-tiered tower that arose from its center. One-story wings stretched out on either side.

The stone face was mottled, corroded, ravaged by time, but even at this distance was still impressive—a monument to the wealth, power, and creative energy that had constructed it some two thousand years ago.

Bolan panned the length of the structure. The ornate facade of the temple bore several carved faces of what was probably Buddha, all wearing the same enigmatic smile. The walls were decorated with vigorous carvings of humans, animals, and gods.

Bolan scanned the area that he could see immediately surrounding the temple, taking in the line of pagodas that dotted the stretch of ground between the far side of the river and the structure itself.

He thought again of the strange contradictions of this land.

During some two and a half centuries of sustained and fervent piety, in an age when much of Europe was sunk in anarchy, kings and commoners together had spent their wealth honoring Buddha in this land.

The best architects, masons and sculptors of Southeast Asia had combined their unmatched skill to construct countless shrines such as this one. Bolan recalled the story of one harsh king who reportedly had threatened to execute the bricklayer responsible if a needle could slide between any two unmortared bricks in his pagoda.

But though their tributes to Buddha were timeless and enduring, as were the teachings of Buddha himself, the advanced civilization and culture that had produced these shrines was but a dim memory today.

The saffron-robed Buddhist monks who had studied, prayed and taught within those walls—as well as the hordes of courtiers, artisans, scholars, merchants and laborers who had visited them here—had long since disappeared.

Many such temples had been completely enveloped by the jungle, up until the early part of this century when French archaeologists began uncovering and restoring the architectural masterpieces.

Yeah, thought Bolan. *Timeless...and yet as changeable as everything else in this violent corner of the world.*

The camouflage was indeed near perfect. It would have to be, to fool those who traveled this river during daylight hours.

But yeah, times *had* changed. And that building across the Sông Hong was no longer a temple. It was the maximum-security military prison that held Colonel Bob McFee.

It was Bolan's objective.

His last area of interest was the chain-link fence that ran the full perimeter of the temple's "front yard," parallel to the riverbank, about twenty yards up a slight incline of tall grass.

His inspection complete, Bolan replaced the Starlight in the waterproof pouch—along with the Beretta and the AutoMag and several grenades, now removed from his person. He put his other gear, garottes and stilettos, on the ground.

Then he stripped down, placing his clothes in the pouch, preparing for the swim to the other side. He stood without clothes.

"I'm leaving the AKM and the rest of my gear with you," Bolan told the headman. "I'll be traveling light. Give me thirty minutes from now to get back."

"Low building to right is where prisoners are kept," the Meo replied. "Do you think McFee kept somewhere else?"

"There's a good chance of it," Bolan grunted. "With what McFee knows, he'll be top-secret material. I doubt if the army will want him mingling with their run-of-the mill prisoners."

"General Trang is commander of prison," said Sioung. "A very clever man. A very evil man. It is as you say. McFee would not be in the obvious place. Trang would see to that. But what if you do not return within thirty minutes, Colonel?"

"Then I won't be coming back at all," Bolan

replied. "And you'll have to come up with another plan."

He lifted a brief wave in farewell and started to turn away, carrying the waterproof pouch.

Sioung checked that move by saying, "American, wait. I have one more thing to say."

Bolan paused as the Mont picked up a stick from the ground. Sioung etched an outline in the dirt between the two men.

Bolan was not surprised at what he saw sketched by the stick in the loose earth near his feet.

Sioung had traced a rough drawing of a marksman's medal.

"Hello, Sioung," Bolan said simply.

Sioung spoke with a trembling voice. "The face of a man can change. The soul cannot, and the eyes are the window to the soul. I can see you, Sergeant Mercy, and I would see you through a thousand faces. May the gods hurry you back to us safely— Colonel Phoenix."

Sioung did not expect a reply. He turned away from Bolan and moved to rejoin the others.

There was no more time.

The Executioner moved out, naked, at a low trot toward the riverbank, carrying the pouch containing arms and clothing.

No, he was not surprised.

These were, yeah, Mack Bolan's kind of people.

But these were also the final minutes before this mission went *hard*. The American warrior's combat consciousness was already accelerating, jumping ahead to what lay before him.

Bolan was a penetration specialist. There would necessarily be some ad-libbing once he reached the other side of the river. And chances to take.

But he would get inside.

Busting *in* was only half the game, however.

Busting *out*—that would be something else again.

8

Bolan emerged from the dark waters of the Sông Hong. The big nude figure kept low, melding with the deep shadows along the riverbank.

In the short time it had taken him to swim across the river, the morning fog had lifted another two feet. He would have to move fast. The chill of the river water spurred him on.

Bolan quickly suited up. He stretched out prone and unsheathed the Starlight spotting scope. He would make one final pan of his objective before moving in.

Some sixty feet of knee-high elephant grass separated him from the chain-link fence that surrounded the prison grounds.

He now took passing interest to the terrain beyond the temple, which he had been unable to make out from his angle across the river.

Flatlands stretched out past the temple, dotted by only occasional clumps of trees. Farther in the distance Bolan saw the tower and blinking amber light of the army base airstrip. Beyond it he could discern only the vague shapes of barracks and warehouses, these perhaps one and a half kilometers to the rear of the temple. That would be the army depot itself.

He brought the infrared sighting scope back to the temple grounds. Specifically to the line of "pagodas" that occupied the sloping area between the fence and prison.

Each pagoda was topped by a TV camera mounted on pivots. Each TV camera eyed an arc of forty-five degrees.

Bolan spent a precious minute watching those cameras as they watched the ground that he had to traverse.

The chill caused shivers to course through his body. But he ignored the cold. He had eyes only for the scanning range of the cameras on the two pagodas that were nearest him.

These were the cameras he would have to dodge.

He ascertained the length of time each camera would be focused away from his intended angle of approach.

Then he moved out.

He stashed the Starlight back under his belt. Keeping low, his iced blue eyes never ceasing to scan their surroundings, the penetration specialist beelined away from the riverbank. He moved through the grass, slick with dew, toward the chain-link fence.

He reached the fence and crouched his bulk down against it. As he had expected, he heard the faint, steady hum that told him the fence was electrified.

From a packet on his belt, Bolan removed a pair of

standard alligator clips connected by a five-foot length of electrician's wire. Bolan connected each clip to a point on the fence on either side of him, rerouting the electrical current so that a four-foot gap in the fence in front of him was uncharged.

Two quick hand-pulls, and the Executioner was over.

He dropped to the opposite side of the fence, landing in a low combat-ready crouch with the Beretta Brigadier now snug in his right fist.

He moved like hell and reached the base of the nearest pagoda without being detected by either of the nearest TV cameras.

Bolan paused in the shadows of the structure, tumbling the number count off in his mind as he waited for his next break. He fanned the eerie predawn light around him with eyes and Beretta.

There was no movement.

The temple. The pagodas. The mist. The cold silence.

That was all.

Now!

He made the last dash from the pagoda across another fifty yards to the base of the temple's main tower center-section. As he made the sprint, he threw a backward glance.

All right!

He had timed his run right on schedule. Again he had eluded the panning gaze of the rotating cameras.

He came to a stop and paused beneath the ferocious head of a tiger, carved into a protruding stone arch.

Bolan heard footsteps.

Someone approaching.

He flattened himself against the wall, behind the arch bearing the stone tiger's head. One cold eye gazed around that arch, waiting for those footsteps, which were approaching from beyond the veil of mist along a gravel maintenance road that passed this spot.

Bolan raised the Beretta.

He was ready to kill.

A man in a light-green Viet guard uniform, including circular sun helmet and button-flap side-arm holster, emerged from the shimmering mist.

The short guy toted a Soviet AK-47 assault rifle strapped over his narrow shoulder. He was just finishing off a smoke.

The guard's attitude and manner saved his life. Bolan relaxed his finger from the Beretta's trigger.

Soft probes like this always worked best in the hour near dawn when the guards who had been on duty all night were tired and careless, bored after a long, uneventful night.

The guard took a final drag on his cigarette, tossed the butt away, and strolled toward the brick wall some twelve feet to Bolan's left.

The guard pushed one of the bricks in the wall.

A disguised door swung inward.

Bolan had wondered where the front entrance to the prison was located. Now he knew.

Before the guard had time to step all the way through the doorway, another sound emerged from out there in the morning fog.

An approaching automobile.

The guard stepped back out onto the gravel road. Within moments a sleek, chauffeured Russian-manufactured ZIL military staff car slid to a purring stop alongside the entrance.

The guard was waiting at attention as if he had been there all along.

The Oriental chauffeur emerged from behind the wheel. He circled around the car and held the rear door open for the passenger: a Viet in his mid-forties, clothed in civvies, smoking a cigarette, with an air of impatience and authority about him.

The new arrival hurried past the soldier, returning the guard's salute with a barely perceptible nod, then disappeared through the doorway leading into the prison. The guard followed, closing the door behind them.

The chauffeur returned to the car, brought the vehicle around in a smooth U-turn, and drove off the way he had come.

Bolan moved away from the archway. He crept along the base of the temple toward the doorway. He was looking for the point close to the ground where the TV cameras on top of the pagodas would be linking up their lines to the main building. His intention was to tamper with the linkup when he found it, to disrupt in some way the reception at the security post inside. At which point a guard would be dispatched, hopefully through that doorway. And then he would improvise his way inside.

After witnessing the arrival of the VIP in the ZIL limo, Bolan wanted into the building especially fast. He was curious to learn who this new arrival was. What was the VIP's business here?

Did it concern Bob McFee?

Did it concern Mack Bolan?

Bolan had just slipped past the hidden entrance to the temple when he heard the door begin to open again.

He flattened himself against the brick wall. There were no arches to seek cover behind.

Another guard stepped out, also armed with an AK-47 slung over his shoulder, almost casually. The first guard apparently was returning a favor to his buddy, covering for this guard while the guy stepped out for a smoke of his own.

The guard started down the gravel driveway in Bolan's direction. His attention was on the pack of cigarettes in his hands as he extracted a butt even before the door was halfway closed behind him.

He looked up, sticking the smoke between his lips—just as Bolan came at him with a hard chop that caught the guy just below his left ear, rendering him unconscious immediately. The guard would have no idea what had happened.

In one fast motion Bolan caught him and eased him out of casual sight behind some tall, untrimmed grass along the base of the wall. The guy would be out of it for at least an hour, hopefully giving Bolan time to get in and out, and when he came to, the guard could well be too groggy to remember having seen anything at all—or too mystified, or afraid to talk about it because it indicated he had been away from his post inside. Bolan could have killed the guard easily enough, but the primary concern on a soft probe was that it stay soft. Dead bodies lying around were always a problem, whereas "sleeping" bodies, if discovered, could be written off to laxity on the part of the guards themselves.

Only splintered seconds had passed since the guard had stepped out for his smoke. The door he'd left behind was still easing shut.

An inch before it closed, Bolan caught the door panel with his fingertips. He eased it back open a few more inches and slipped inside.

He found himself in a guardroom. It looked like the security base station for the prison.

It was obvious at a glance that the Viets had thoroughly gutted the temple and reconstructed its insides into a modern, functional concrete building.

But at 0510 hours on this bleak morning, the security personnel were decidedly not functioning at maximum efficiency.

The first Viet guard was the only person in the room. He sat at one of the two consoles that took up opposite walls of the station. He was idly watching a bank of TV screens, monitoring the cameras outside, too occupied with electronic security to notice the real thing as it moved wraithlike behind him.

A corridor lined with offices stretched off beyond the guardroom—one of the single-story extended wings of the "temple" as seen from outside. It was the administrative wing of the prison.

As he soundlessly left the guardroom and slid into the corridor, Bolan sighted the VIP in civvies.

The man had paused before a doorway midway down the corridor. He didn't see Bolan. He knocked on the door, opened it almost at once, and stepped from sight.

Bolan moved toward that office door as he heard it snap shut behind the VIP. He hoped to do some eavesdropping. A water cooler stood a few feet short of the door. Bolan was within six feet of it when the door suddenly swung inward again.

In one easy movement, Bolan crouched down out of sight behind the water cooler.

Waiting.

Watching.

The Beretta ready to spit death....

The VIP stepped back into the corridor. He was accompanied by a man in military uniform who wore the rank of a Viet general.

That would be General Trang, the prison commandant.

An interesting pair.

Bolan surreptitiously watched as the two men walked off down the corridor away from him.

This was it. The general and the VIP could be on their way to interrogate McFee. It played, yeah. The general wanted to keep McFee isolated from the regular prisoners in the other wing. A special cell at the far end of the administrative wing made sense.

At the far end of the corridor, the general and the civilian paused before the last door on the right, thirty feet beyond the last office in the hallway in a cul-de-sac with no exits.

General Trang was big for a Vietnamese. His simplest gesture carried a brute animal directness. Animal, yeah.

He reached into the tunic of his uniform, withdrew a key and unlocked the door. Then he and the VIP disappeared into the room. The door closed behind them.

Silence enveloped the corridor, the prison. Within minutes the building would be waking. But not yet.

Bolan reached the door only moments after it clicked shut behind them. It was made of heavy steel, not at all like the others lining the corridor. Centered at eye level in the door was a rectangular window covered by wire mesh.

Bolan ducked below the viewing window. He gently tried the door. It was locked. He inched an eye up to a corner of the mesh window and peered inside.

At first, from his limited vantage point, he could see only General Trang and the civilian. They were exchanging sharp, heated words that Bolan could not hear.

But he was able to read the relationship between those two men at a glance. Bolan had some understanding of how the government in this country worked. The civilian was most likely General Trang's political party counterpart in overseeing the administration of this prison facility. And there was bad blood between them. Bolan realized as he studied the two Vietnamese that they hated each other's guts, but because of circumstances they had to work together whether they liked it or not.

Bolan watched Trang and the other man for only a few moments. Then he shifted his body and, remaining low, peered into the room at a different angle.

And yeah, this was it.

Bolan had found Bob McFee.

9

McFee winced through the throbbing pain between his temples, caused by the simple act of parting his eyelids.

His eyes widened into nothing more than narrow slits in his battered face. There was no way he was going to advertise to his captors that he was conscious. But they had grilled him so much over the past four days that even the slightest physical exertion caused agony.

He probably didn't look like much on the outside, he knew. He was hanging shackled from the wall. But inside, Bob McFee felt a warm glow of pride.

The bastards hadn't gotten a thing from him!

Not so far. And they weren't about to. Let the sadistic little creeps do what they wanted. They had already sent in three separate pros to interrogate him. And they had learned absolutely nothing.

Not that they didn't know their shit. They did. And then some. The interrogators had obviously been men whose specialty was torture and not a damn thing else.

They had used matches on Bob McFee. They had

beaten him. They had broken the fingers on his right hand. They had pulled the fingernails out from the left.

One of the "interrogators" had been skilled in the use of metal bars and straps, skilled at twisting a man into all sorts of distorting positions to induce pain, knowing just how far to bend arms and legs without breaking limbs.

But no, by God, they hadn't broken him. McFee had been tortured on two other occasions. He hadn't broken those times, either. And he had "interrogated" other men. He understood about the numb half-death *beyond* pain, which was held there in reserve by some grace of the nervous system. If one could just hold on to the point when the pain was not *hot*, no matter what they did.... The pain itself anesthetized you until you felt nothing. Then all they could do was kill you or let you alone to heal up for a few days, so they could get to work again on the wounds and the bruises.

McFee had been pushed over the line to that point of numbness all over. He knew it—and he was pretty damn sure that his Viet interrogators knew it, too.

Question: what would they do next?

He was in a cell that had a high ceiling and no windows. There was a linoleum floor. A large, bare table stood directly in front of McFee. The table on which much of his torture had taken place. It was stained with his blood, and with the blood of others.

What had brought McFee around to consciousness was the sound of a key being turned in the lock of his cell door. He had never lost the ability to rest in the kind of half-sleep that every soldier in a combat zone learned if he wished to stay alive.

He had not allowed himself to slip into a truly deep sleep since his capture. Even now, his senses heavy from the numbing effect of all he had been through, he was able to place a corner of his brain on alert.

He watched now as the cell door swung inward.

Two men stepped into the cell. General Trang and the civilian party member, Nguyen Vinh. They approached the wall where McFee hung shackled.

He had been stripped naked that first day. He sagged from the chains—bolted into the cold concrete wall—that held his arms in a painful position up and out from him. Two more shackles around his ankles suspended him several inches above the floor.

So it's Mutt-and-Jeff time again, thought McFee groggily. Neither of these two had as yet taken a personal hand in McFee's interrogation. But they appeared to be overseeing the whole thing.

McFee had overheard some of their conversation in the past. He was fluent in Vietnamese, having operated out of this corner of the world for so long. He knew that the prison commandant and the man from Hanoi didn't get along at all. The party liaison appeared to disdain the necessity of physical torture, and too the less than subtle enjoyment that the general seemed to get from watching pain inflicted.

General Trang eyed McFee closely as he and Vinh came to a stop before the shackled man.

"Are you awake, American?"

McFee had closed his eyes again.

Vinh spoke in a worried voice. "Perhaps he is dead. Perhaps the last session with your man was too much for him."

"He is not dead," snarled Trang. "Wake up, American pig."

McFee's head was smashed backward into the concrete wall as General Trang whapped him full force with an open palm across the right side of his face.

McFee could not stifle a moan of pain. With that much out, he went ahead and forced his eyelids apart.

"'Morning, warden."

Trang backhanded the left side of McFee's bruised, lacerated face. The American's head again smashed into the wall. McFee's vision grew blurry for several seconds. But he fought back unconsciousness.

Had this been like the other interrogation sessions, he would have welcomed gladly the slide into dark nothingness. But this was different. This was the first time Trang and Vinh had deigned to question him personally.

This had to mean something.

"I am not interested in your bullshit American wisecracks," spat Trang. His eyes flickered with a light that wasn't sane as he pushed his face to within inches of McFee's. "You may think that you are not expendable," he hissed. "But you are, Colonel. Others out there hold the same information that you possess. We will apprehend them eventually, as we did you. If you talk, it will be easier for you—and for us. But this is your final chance. Will you tell us what you know about the Montagnard underground?"

McFee didn't think he had the strength left in him, but he summoned up all his energy and got it out.

"Piss up a rope, Fu Manchu."

Trang reared back in a manner that reminded McFee of a cat baring its fangs. The general reached for a side arm that rode at his hip. He yanked out pistol, a 9mm Soviet Stetchin.

Trang was bringing the pistol butt down toward McFee's forehead.

"I have had enough of your insolence, American pig!"

McFee closed his eyes for the death blow.

Which did not come.

He opened his eyes, the pain momentarily forgotten in the heat of the moment.

Nguyen Vinh had stepped between McFee and General Trang. The little politico had some backbone after all. Vinh reached up with both hands and stopped the downward arc of Trang's arm.

"General! I insist that you control yourself, in the name of the People's Republic!"

With one mighty tug Trang yanked his arm free of Vinh. But he did not continue his assault on McFee. He took a step backward. He did not holster the Stetchin.

The general glared at McFee as he spoke to Vinh. His face was a dark mask of barely controlled rage.

"I think I shall advise Hanoi in my next communiqué that their man in the field seems to be doing his best to hamper a most important investigation."

Vinh relaxed also. He stepped away from the American.

"That is your prerogative, General. But until then, we shall continue this interrogation in a more civil fashion. I have stood by and watched enough inhumane treatment inflicted upon this man."

"You sympathize with the American pig, then? Hanoi will be most interested to hear that as well," said Trang.

"No, I don't sympathize with him," Vinh replied in steady tones. "My wife and family were killed during the Christmas bombing of '72. My mother died of starvation in Haiphong during the American blockade there." He looked at McFee with emotionless eyes. "I have no love for this man, General. But I have witnessed enough savagery in my lifetime to last me forever. We are not savages, General. This is a delicate intelligence matter. This man must be properly interrogated in Hanoi. You have accomplished nothing here. I will not allow anger to rule the day."

Trang holstered his Stetchin.

"Very well, Mr. Vinh. Anger shall *not* rule the day."

He reached into the pocket of his tunic and withdrew an object inlaid with pearl. It was the handle of a folding knife. Trang snapped open the knife with a jerk of his wrist. The nine-inch blade glinted in the overhead light.

Vinh stepped forward, raising a cautionary hand.

"General, please—"

Trang stopped the Hanoi man with a stare and a tone of voice that were menacingly quiet.

"I'm warning you, Vinh. Do not interfere. I am military commander of this facility. This interrogation is my direct responsibility until Hanoi decrees otherwise. This man has vital information that I need. I will now proceed with the questioning."

"General, Hanoi—"

"Hanoi be damned," growled Trang. "Stay out of my way, Vinh, or you won't be reporting anything to Hanoi." He turned to face McFee. He stepped forward. The knife was held pointed forward at chest level. As he stepped closer, Trang began rotating the blade in small circles. "Now, my fine American pig. We will stick you in places you have not been stuck before and see how you squeal. You will speak to me then... or you will know more pain than you have ever known in your life."

McFee closed his eyes again. He placed his tongue between his teeth, ready to do some biting. Sure, most of his body was beyond feeling. But the general sounded like a man who kept his word when he said he was going to cause a person some pain.

Colonel Robert McFee did his best to escape the horrible reality of that moment by shifting his conscious mind to something else entirely, with the hope that the pain would make him black out soon.

He thought again, as he had every day for the past eight years since he had lost her, of his Phan Thi. His beloved Phan Thi. He had met her when he was stationed in Saigon during the war and she was a civilian worker on the base.

Phan Thi had been the most beautiful, intelligent, sensitive woman that Bob McFee had ever known. They fell in love. They married. She had borne him a son.

Bob McFee had been on a deep-cover mission with the Meo in Laos when the Americans had pulled out of Vietnam. He could have returned to Saigon in time for evacuation easily enough. But it would have meant aborting the mission with the Meos—and the subsequent massacre of at least four villages by Communist troops.

Bob had not pulled out. He stayed on and saw the mission through, American withdrawal or no, just as he had been ordered during the top-priority briefing that had seen him off on the mission.

So Bob McFee had become one of the two thousand or so men who had stayed or been left behind during those frantic days of America's evacuation.

After completion of his mission, he made it back undercover to Saigon as soon as he could. But the summary trial and execution of American collaborators and sympathizers in that city had already begun.

Despite the conquerors' vigorous denial in the world press, thousands had been rounded up and slaughtered. No one knew what became of McFee's son. If the boy was lucky, he had ended up in one of the hundreds of indoctrination camps set up across the country. *If* the child was lucky....

McFee had returned to Laos and, subsequently, North Vietnam, working with the Montagnards; with most of them he shared a strong mutual respect rooted in his extensive work alongside them during the war.

And now it was about to end in this fetid torture chamber somewhere in the Red River Delta! Shackled to the wall as he was, Bob McFee didn't see a damn thing in hell that he could do about it except transcend the moment until death came, and to die with dignity.

But the knife did not touch him.

McFee opened his eyes. All sorts of things must have shone in them. Trang was standing there, watching, just waiting to get some reaction like this, like a cat playing with a mouse.

When Trang saw the symphony of fear, confusion,

and hope in McFee's eyes, the general started laughing like an idiot. He moved in again. The knife lowered now toward McFee's genitals.

Nguyen Vinh was pasty white. He seemed to be trembling as he turned away from the scene between Trang and McFee to stand facing a wall, his trembling back to them.

"And now, my American friend, you will tell us everything we want to know about the Montagnards." Trang's voice was a whisper as cold as the touch of the knife. "I shall begin with your—"

At that precise moment, an eruption of sound exploded from the outside corridor.

Trang pulled the blade back an inch and glanced over his shoulder.

The disturbance was the shouted command of a Viet guard from out in the hallway, followed by the shrill blast of a whistle—the guard sounding the alert.

Bob McFee wondered vaguely what the hell was going on. He sensed Trang and Vinh both uttering exclamations and shifting their attention to the bolted entrance to the room.

But a human body, even the toughest, can withstand only so much. The tortured American shackled to the wall had again been pushed beyond the emotional limits of endurance.

McFee felt the dark chamber of horrors begin to swirl around his head. Panic gripped him, the residue of emotional shock. He willed himself to resist the sudden sense of darkness closing in on him. But he could not.

The commotion around him faded.

Colonel Robert McFee slipped into the black well of unconsciousness.

10

Mack Bolan eyeballed the two guards at the instant that they saw him. They had stepped out from one of the offices lining the corridor.

Bolan's battle senses flared him into movement.

Both Viets had swung their assault rifles down and out at waist level into firing position, eyes popping wide with the adrenaline rush of this unexpected confrontation.

The guard to Bolan's left shouted out a command for him to halt where he was. The guard to his right fumbled to get at a whistle chained to his tunic, even as he tried to aim his AK-47 at Bolan.

But a Beretta was already tracking into the fray.

The guards released one good shout and one good whistle. Then Bolan was squeezing off rounds, muting these two forever.

The guard to his left had his mouth open wide to repeat the barked command. He fielded a 9mm projectile through the mouth instead. There was no entry wound: but as the man went into his tumbling death dance, his head became wreathed in a gory mist from what must have been one massive exit wound.

Guard number two let the whistle drop from his mouth. He was still pulling up his AK-47 on Bolan when the Beretta's second messenger of death punched his right eyeball out through the back of his head.

Bolan tossed a glance through the wire mesh of the door to the cell that held Bob McFee and his interrogators.

The civilian VIP in the room had turned from the wall and was looking around at the door.

General Trang also had spun around in Bolan's direction. And Bolan was now aware that if discovery by those two guards had cost him the "softness" of this probe, then it had also granted Bob McFee a reprieve from the castrator's knife.

Trang snapped the knife shut and pocketed it. He was grabbing his holstered side arm. He seemed to have forgotten about McFee shackled to the wall.

Bolan's gut knotted with cold rage. It was essential to the mission that he get Bob McFee out alive, so that McFee could return to Washington with the massive store of data he carried in his head regarding the whereabouts of all the other POWs.

Sure, Bolan could blast his way into the hellhole right now. But he would only be kissing his and McFee's lives goodbye. Those shackles holding McFee were secure in the concrete of the wall. And the prison was already alerted to Bolan's presence.

He swung away from the door, intent on getting the hell out of there and on with the final phase of the mission: busting McFee out in one piece.

The blank walls that were the cul-de-sac of this end of the corridor stared back at him blankly, offering no way out. He started down the corridor toward the first office doorway. He leaped over the corpses of the two guards and almost made that doorway thirty feet away—when two more guards appeared down at the end of the corridor, in the archway leading to the security station.

Both soldiers fell into prone firing positions.

Bolan squeezed off two rounds from hip level even as he flung himself back against the wall. He scored a head hit. One of the army regulars sported a jagged black dot in the center of his forehead when he landed.

The other guard, the one Bolan had first crept past in the guardroom, made it into a belly flop and immediately opened up with his RPK at where the big man in combat black had been standing a moment ago.

The heavy yammering of the weapon was deafening in the narrow confines of the hallway. The 7.62mm projectiles zipped along the corridor. Bolan felt their breeze.

Another green-uniformed guard appeared. The guy fell into a crouching firing position as soon as he grasped the situation, beginning to swing his AK-47 at Bolan's position against the wall.

Meanwhile an alarm system began emitting a shrill discordant howl throughout the building.

Bolan was unclipping from his belt the stun grenade he had brought across the river with him. Then he hurled the missile underarm down the length of the corridor. He turned to face the wall.

The two guards caught the full effect of the blinding flash and hellish roar. The power of the blast tossed them back into the walls of the corridor. It literally stunned them out of their minds. The explosion would keep the general and his liaison man frozen in their tracks near McFee's cell.

Bolan continued on toward the doorway he had initially been heading for. He kicked the wood panel off its hinges and entered, the Beretta tracking for something to kill. The hysteria of the alarm jangled in his ears.

The office was dark, deserted. There was another door leading out through the opposite wall.

Bolan closed the hallway door behind him. The sudden quiet in the office was a relief. He crossed to the other door, opened it—and stepped outside into the early-morning light. This second doorway was camouflaged on the outside by one of the stone arches of the "temple."

Bolan started away from the building toward the fence and the river. But he immediately fell into a combat crouch when he and four Viet army regulars—who came running along the gravel drive fronting the building—spotted each other at the same time.

The guards fanned out.

Bolan stretched the Belle out before him in a two-handed firing stance and picked off a couple of the men with rapid, coolly placed rounds that splattered the smiling face of a carved Buddha behind them with exploding dead matter. It was as Buddha would have prophesied.

The other two guards dodged behind an abutment and commenced pulling off wild, barely placed shots. But they were close enough.

Bolan fell back behind the archway that camouflaged the door. Slugs whistled and ricocheted off the arch.

He fed a fresh clip into the Beretta's grip, then made a dash from the cover of the arch toward the end corner of the administrative wing, some ten yards away.

More slugs from the two guards whistled above and alongside him, but he made the end of the building and sprinted around it, deliberately gaining speed as if to launch a long-range run for cover.

He suddenly stopped, then gave the guards behind him a quick ten count. He stepped out to meet them head-on. His reading of their response was accurate. They were tearing along the wall of the building in hot pursuit, assuming that Bolan had cut around the corner and kept going.

The Executioner squeezed off two rounds. The shots slipped the guards into hell, their path from this world slick with the gore of scum.

The prison alarm system was still broadcasting its shrill screech over the area.

Bolan could see more guards emerging from the security station midway down the building. He would never make it to the river on foot from this angle.

He continued on his way around the wing of the temple, toward the rear grounds of the structure.

Not knowing how he would get out.

11

Bolan gained the rear grounds of the temple-prison, which up to now had been blocked from his sight. He met no resistance. There was no sign of army troops—yet.

He saw that a third wing stretched out from the rear of the main temple structure. This wing, one story like the other two, had not been visible from the river.

A loading dock that could accommodate two trucks was visible halfway down the length of it. At the moment only one truck, a four-ton ZIL150, stood there idling with its bed backed up to the dock but with tailgate raised.

A uniformed driver was signing something for another guy on the loading dock. The two seemed disturbed by the ruckus out front; they were moving fast. The driver left the dock and walked briskly toward the cab of his truck.

The scene was bathed in the warmth of a new dawn. The sun was a bloodred disk riding low in the eastern sky. The fog had lifted except for the mist that shrouded the distant hills. Dew sparkled like diamonds amid the grassy flatland separating Bolan from the dock.

The Executioner moved with silent speed along the wall of the temple until he reached a spot twenty feet short of the loading dock. The run had taken only seconds. Neither of the men had seen him.

The driver climbed into the truck and slid behind the steering wheel. He turned and leaned out the window as if to call something back to the man on the loading dock. He saw Bolan.

The Beretta spat silent fire. The man went rigid behind the wheel, then slipped from sight.

Bolan ran toward the cab, finally coming into view of the man on the dock. The man shouted. Three more men, armed with AK-47s, came running from the shadows beyond the loading apron.

Bolan paused to peg off two rounds that kicked two men out of this life.

One man sprawled out flat on his back. The other was slammed into a wall under the impact of the 9mm projectile, then careened forward again and over the edge of the dock, pitching down to the tarmac where he didn't move. The other two men fell away for cover.

Bolan yanked open the truck cab door and tossed the corpse onto the ground behind him. He took the man's place behind the wheel.

He reached forward, twisted the ignition key and slammed the four-tonner into gear, tearing away from there like a hot bullet toward the gravel road, which he estimated would lead around toward the front of the building again.

Toward the river.

Two men back on the loading dock opened fire. Their rounds stitched harmlessly into the truck's rear end.

Bolan steered the rig on two wheels around the far end of the temple wing, kicking up a muddy cloud of dirt and gravel behind him. He ran into no resistance until the gravel road linked up with the one that traversed the front grounds of the temple, the one that separated Bolan from the river.

Those front grounds were overrun with soldiers.

A full guard squad, twelve men in all, was swarming out the doorway to the security section. They were dividing up as they hit the gravel driveway out front. Half the men were deploying toward the administrative wing of the building, away from Bolan. The other six were running with weapons at high port toward the opposite wing of the building.

Straight into Mack Bolan.

He shifted the rig into high, tromped the gas pedal to the floor and rammed ahead at full speed.

There was barely time for two of the men to dodge out of the way. Of the other four, two had time to raise their weapons and squeeze off one round apiece at the truck that had careened around the corner and was bearing down on them.

Twin holes spiderwebbed cracks into the windshield inches to Bolan's right. He felt a flying shard of glass slice across his right cheek.

Then the giant four-ton was thudding into those who had not had time to jump aside. Heavy metal traumatized the life from human bodies, toppling the bodies down and under the truck, where the rolling tires ground them into pulp.

Bolan yanked the rig's steering wheel to the left.

His only hope, he knew, was to traverse the front "temple" grounds to the bank of the river, where he could ditch the truck and swim to the other side for rendezvous with the Meos.

His ears were filled with the throaty roar of the truck's engine as he left the gravel road and curved off between a pair of the pagodas. The rig rocked and shimmied around Bolan as he sent it roaring down the sloping field in the direction of the chain-link fence that stretched along the perimeter of the prison grounds four hundred yards away.

The steady yammer of rifle and machine-gun fire sounded behind him. But the more distance he gained toward the river, the wilder the rounds became, the less sharp the sound of their aim.

With three hundred yards to go, closing in on the fence at 65 mph, Bolan figured he was just about clear. But with a rush of adrenaline his peripheral vision registered two smaller, three-quarter-ton ZIL trucks that were sailing in, bouncing at full speed across the bumpy terrain from opposite ends of the prison building. The trucks were on courses obviously intended to intercept Bolan before he reached the chain-link fence.

Both pursuing trucks carried three men in the bed. Each man toted what looked like a RPK from this distance, and two men—one in the bed of each truck—were already aiming at Bolan's rig, using the cabs of their trucks to draw aim.

Bolan tried to feed his truck more gas. But he was coaxing all the speed he could from her.

The pursuing trucks were lighter and faster. They cleared the pagodas and started closing in fast on him.

A gunner opened up when the truck on the left was some fifteen yards off and still closing.

Bolan heard the thundering roar of the machine gun and the fainter punching sounds as slugs stitched their way in a line across the vehicle's chassis, tracking forward.

He didn't slacken his speed. But he did hunch low behind the wheel, losing his steering vision entirely for a while below the dash, as glass and metal only inches above him were pulverized by a brief hot stream of flying lead.

When the fire ceased, he straightened and with the same movement tracked the mighty .44 AutoMag up and out from where it rode on his right hip.

Bolan was taking quick aim through the truck's side window. Then Big Thunder thundered bigger than ever. The machine gunner's chest exploded inward, bathing those behind him in a shower of life juices.

Another round shattered the window in front of the driver's seat—and shattered the head of its driver—leaving the speeding truck to swerve wildly out of control on the rough earth.

Bolan had a vague impression of the truck over-ending and bodies tossing through the air. But his main attention was already focused on the second truck, closing in on his right flank.

Bolan and the surviving truckload of soldiers were angling at trajectories that would intercept one hundred feet before Bolan's rig reached the fence.

In his rearview mirror, Bolan saw the guy propping his RPK across the cab of the vehicle. He was trying like hell to get steady enough for a burst as the truck jounced over the slope.

The reasonable thing for Bolan to do was to steer away from his pursuers at a new angle in an effort to put a little more distance between them.

Reasonable, sure.

But Bolan preferred something else.

He slackened his speed, downshifted, and yanked the steering wheel slightly to the left and then mightily to the right.

It was the last thing the driver of the pursuing truck saw. The maneuver had planted Bolan's truck directly in the path of his pursuer.

Bolan heard a cry that was in fact a frightened scream.

The truck plowed head-on into the side of Bolan's rig with the terrible sound of impacting metal. The power of the collision ripped the steering wheel from Bolan's control and pushed the four-ton into a sudden tilt.

His ears still ringing with the crunch of wrenched metal, Bolan released his hands from the steering wheel. He reached up and grabbed the door frame on the passenger side. He pressed the door open. He pulled himself up and out of the cab as the truck began listing onto its side.

He hit the ground, his senses still reeling from the crash.

His truck tipped over onto the chain-link fence with such power that it flattened the fence. The ground near the bed of the truck was littered with cardboard boxes that had been the truck's cargo.

What had been the pursuing vehicle was now an unsettling sight. The driver had gone into the steering column and windshield, rendering him a dead mess. Two soldiers lay tossed across the sides of the flat-bed, their torsos twisted at impossible angles.

One soldier had been thrown free. He was dazedly pulling himself up from where he had landed twenty feet away, badly shaken and not at all sure of where he was. Before he had a chance to figure it out, Bolan negated the guy with a head shot from the AutoMag.

As the sounds of warfare and full-throttle vehicles faded, Bolan could still hear the jangling alarm system from the prison. He looked up the sloping ground and made out the forms of more soldiers advancing from between the line of pagodas.

But they were still some three hundred yards away. Still far enough away for Bolan to make the riverbank.

With as little time as he had, however, some instinct made the Executioner gamble away another few seconds.

He stooped down beside one of the littered boxes from the bed of the truck. He wondered why there had been men loading the truck well before most of the prison was even awake. Why the secrecy?

He quickly found out.

The one box that he examined was full of drycleaned Viet army uniforms. Packed between the uniforms, making a barely noticeable bulge, was a plastic packet weighing about one kilo that was packed tight with a pure white powder.

Bolan broke the bag, dabbed a moist fingertip into the powder, and touched the end of his tongue. It was raw heroin. After being cut or whatever, that kilo would carry a street value in the millions in any country in the world. . . .

Then he was up and quitting the scene, moving briskly over the truck, over the flattened length of fence, hurtling in a low dash toward the river.

Some of the troops back up the slope opened fire at him. But they were too far away for accurate shooting.

Bolan reached the bank of the Sông Hong. He rapidly stripped down again, repacking the waterproof pouch. Then he hit the water in a clean dive that propelled him on his way out of there.

It was too early for the river to be teeming with the congestion of commerce that would be clogging it by midday. There were a few craft far upriver, but nothing between him and the opposite bank. Nothing, that is, except precious time and space. In no time there would be choppers and patrol boats from the army depot out looking for him.

Bolan's powerful arms and legs sped him smoothly through the water. He did not look back.

So there was a new twist to this already twisted situation.

General Trang was dealing in illegal drugs. And it was a sizable operation. Bolan was willing to bet that there had been other packets of white powder in other boxes of Viet fatigues supposedly being shipped out of the prison laundry. And the bag that Bolan had seen alone would have fetched a cool million or more from any drug wholesaler in the States.

Bolan wondered if—how—he could make this new piece of information fit into the scheme of what he had to accomplish here today.

One thing was for damn sure.

He would have to move fast.

Bob McFee was still priority number one.

Sure, the "soft" probe having gone "hard" had made things even tougher for Mack Bolan. But at least he had made it outside those prison walls.

Not so the American fighting man who was shackled to the wall of his torture chamber inside that unholy "temple" of the damned.

Yeah, the Executioner would have to move *damn* fast.

He did his best to ignore the gnawing feeling in his gut that he might already be too late.

12

"Excuse me, sir. You're wanted in the communications shed."

The orderly's words cut in on Jack Grimaldi's thoughts, tugging him from his concern. He looked up, having stared down for too long at the coffee grounds in his cup.

"What time is it, guy?"

"0530 hours, Mr. Grimaldi."

The pilot pushed himself to his feet.

"Lead the way," he said. "Let's see what they've got."

He followed the orderly out of the shack that served as an orderly room. They were at the covert American base secreted away in the mountainous plateau region of northeast Thailand near the Laotian border.

Except for the long arm of cleared land that was the crude landing strip, dense jungle wood grew flush to the handful of shacks and hangars that comprised the base.

The Harrier sat on that landing strip now. Waiting, just as Jack Grimaldi was waiting.

Waiting for word from Bolan.

The camp was manned by a rotating crew of twelve U.S. civilians, ex-Special Forces personnel mostly, who still adhered to paramilitary protocol and these days functioned under top-security clearance as employees of the Thai government. They were responsible for conducting clandestine CIA activities in cooperation with the Thais, which generally included supplying aid to the anti-Communist guerrilla forces that operated throughout Southeast Asia.

It was two hours since Grimaldi had dropped Bolan into the jungle. Those hours had dragged by for the pilot like dying snails.

His orders were to sit on his duff out here in the middle of nowhere until Bolan called in with information for an air strike and pickup at the temple site.

Grimaldi had expected to hear from Mack Bolan by now.

The pilot was worried.

He had a feeling in his gut that something was wrong. And that feeling had tied him up tight.

The man now known as John Phoenix was far more to Jack Grimaldi than merely his superior in the Stony Man Farm operation. Hell, yeah. The guy meant a damn sight more.

Mack Bolan was a brother.

A brother-in-arms.

A magnificent soldier and human being who had all of Grimaldi's respect, love, devotion, sticky as those words might have sounded when spoken aloud.

But Grimaldi didn't give a damn. He would have died for him, if the truth were known.

The world needed a few dozen Mack Bolans, what with the shape things were in. But thank God there was at least *one* of a kind.

Grimaldi walked beside the soldier across the narrow clearing, toward a wood shack that sprouted a tall communications antenna. The sky to the east was brushed with the first warm tints of a new day.

Grimaldi glanced at those rose hues. Who could understand the respect felt by one hellgrounder for another?

Perhaps Grimaldi understood the Executioner better than most. And he had a right to that special understanding. Grimaldi and the big blitz artist had been through plenty since forming their acquaintance during Bolan's Mafia war in the seventies.

Grimaldi thought again of those early encounters between himself and the big guy that some had dubbed Mack the Bastard.

Jack, he'd been at a weird stage in his life then, that's for damn sure. And Mack Bolan had set him right, had given Grimaldi meaning and direction in a life that had been sadly lacking in such things.

Until 1970, Grimaldi had been doing just fine. As an army pilot of warrant officer rank in Nam, he had flown 137 combat missions in helicopters and fixed-wing aircraft of every size and description. He had been awarded the Airman's Medal, the Commendation Medal, and two Purple Hearts.

Only problem was, all of those military awards didn't mean diddly-shit when he returned stateside after eight years of hard service, hoping to return to "normal" civilian life. Finding a good job, finding a good woman, and settling down to the good life had been Grimaldi's game plan upon his discharge. Only it hadn't worked out that way. And the fact that Grimaldi was only one of countless thousands of returning vets in the same condition had not done a thing to ease the situation.

But the closing of employment doors in his face had been just another example of a pervasive alienation he felt. Many people, some of whom had been good friends, had emphatically disapproved of the war and now openly disapproved of Grimaldi himself.

Yeah, there was a lot of that. But there had been still another factor: the ultimate unsettling realization that he had been living in the hellgrounds for just too damn long. The ideal American dream life could *never* belong to him. Society had trained Jack Grimaldi in highly skilled combat capabilities for which it had no use in peacetime.

Grimaldi had, however, been able to find people who were willing to pay for what he knew, which was how to fly anything, anywhere, under any circumstances, and still come out in one piece with the job completed successfully.

These people had retained Grimaldi. They had utilized his services on an increasingly regular basis, in endeavors that Grimaldi had deduced the first time around were illegal.

Of course, that was between his employers and the law. Grimaldi had craved excitement, and his new bosses had given it to him.

A weird time. Of course.

And that was all a lifetime ago.

A lifetime of realization.

Back in Jack's bad days, Bolan had seemed to sense that Grimaldi was one of the walking wounded. Way back then, Bolan must have seen something in the pilot. Mack may have seen something of himself.

Now, today, they were brothers. Damn straight. Jack owed Bolan for making him realize that there was still a war going on. A war that was being fought at some corner of the world at any point during any day. Over things that *meant* something.

Grimaldi had become a trusted Bolan ally in the Executioner's war against the Mafia, against those men—Grimaldi's former bosses—who had been dangerously close to taking over America from within, with insidious tentacles that at one time had reached all the way into the White House itself, systematically biting away at the heart of the American way of life for some fifty years. A foul, cancerous growth on society.

Bolan had opened Grimaldi's eyes to the true horror of the crime scene of which the pilot had become a part.

Bolan also helped Jack Grimaldi realize that there

were indeed uses for a man of Jack's skills and qualifications. That there were still ideals and values worth putting oneself on the line for.

Mack Bolan had shown Jack Grimaldi the road to redemption.

They had been through some damn tight spots during the time since their first meeting. Both stateside and on an increasingly international scale since the Executioner's reincarnation as Colonel Phoenix.

At last the U.S. government had a top-level unit for the express purpose of taking on sensitive, high-priority missions involving the ever increasing terrorist threat, as well as related operations like this one.

Grimaldi was proud to be a member of that unit.

At the moment, he was a very concerned member.

The orderly stepped aside at the doorway to the communications shack, and the pilot moved past him inside.

A crewman sat at a communications rig. He extended a receiver unit mike toward the pilot.

"Stateside is on the scrambler, Mr. Grimaldi."

The pilot grunted a thank-you. He took the receiver and spoke into the scrambler, as the Specialist Fifth Class got up and left the shack.

"This is Grimaldi. Go ahead."

"Jack, this is Hal. How does it look down there?"

Stony Man Farm's liaison with Wonderland on the Potomac came in clearly across the thousands of miles. The miracle of modern communications, thought Grimaldi. He could picture the head fed clearly in his mind's eye, right down to the unlit stogie that would be jutting from the corner of Brognola's mouth as he spoke.

Hal Brognola went way back with Bolan, too. Back to those Mafia days when the fed and the human war machine in black had shared a mutual respect and friendship based on a joint hatred for the Brotherhood and the helplessness of the judicial system in dealing effectively with the Mafia menace. The fed and Mack the Bastard had shared a friendship that had been one for the books.

Grimaldi could clearly hear the concern in Brognola's voice across the scrambler hookup. Brognola was another brother. And, yeah, this was one family that had a whole lot of concern for each other.

"He's in," he told the fed. "I dropped him at 0330 hours. We're waiting on word from him now. Then I fly back in to provide air cover."

"Any complications on the drop?"

"None. Haven't heard from him yet, but it's too early to start worrying."

"How's the weather?"

"Wonderful. Wish you were here."

"Jack..."

"Low cloud cover on the drop, but the weatherfront was moving southeast, so it should be cleared out by now. Perfect for the flight back in."

"All right. Sounds good. Get back to me as soon as it's over, Jack. And good luck."

"Thanks, Hal. Will do."

That was the conversation. The static of the disconnected linkup filled Grimaldi's ears. He replaced the receiver unit and turned to leave the shack and get back to the orderly room for another cup of coffee.

To wait for Mack Bolan's signal on when to come in with air cover for the hit that Bolan and those Meo warriors were going to make on the prison to bust out Bob McFee.

Grimaldi was burning to get out there and pitch in.

He reflected briefly on his short conversation with Brognola. Hal had been all business, too, not letting any personal emotion show through. But Grimaldi wondered. Did Hal have a premonition, too?

Back in the orderly room shed, the pilot poured himself a cup of coffee. He sat down at the table and lit a cigarette.

Come on, Mack, he thought. *Let's hear from you! What the hell's happening out there?*

13

General Trang hung up the phone on his desk. He stood in his office, shaking with a mixture of anger and intense relief. Nguyen Vinh stood nearby. But Trang had managed to keep his end of the phone conversation too ambiguous for the Hanoi politico to understand.

The general's man, Lieutenant Khanh, had just reported confidentially that the cargo had been recovered intact from the truck that the insane foreign commando had just hijacked.

The cargo was intact. This meant so much to the general's peace of mind. More than anything else. Nevertheless he managed to register a grim expression when he turned to face Vinh. It was not difficult. Part of Lieutenant Khanh's report had been of an official nature, and there was much to feel grim about.

"The intruder has escaped us," he barked. "The man disappeared swimming underwater before the helicopters from the base could close in. No one saw him surface on the other side."

"Could he have drowned?" asked Vinh.

Trang snorted.

"Hardly. The man was a professional. You saw him in action. You saw how many men he killed."

The smaller Viet repressed a shiver.

"I saw nothing. I was waiting here the entire time you were trying to apprehend the man. Do you think he will return?"

Trang's face darkened.

"I sincerely *hope* he will return! Whoever that man was, he shall pay dearly for what happened here today. He will be apprehended, and I shall personally attend to his interrogation. He will die very slowly."

"Do you think he was here for the American prisoner?"

"Almost certainly. That is why I think he will return."

"Perhaps he will bring others," Vinh murmured.

"Then we will be ready for them as well." The general started past Vinh toward the office door. "I will supervise our security. The army is sending me additional troops. When our American friend does try something else, he will find himself trapped by far more than he bargained for."

Vinh started to follow. "I will accompany you."

Trang spun around. "No. This is work for men. You will only be in the way."

The Hanoi man flinched from the rebuff as if from a blow. But there was a backbone of steel beneath his mild manner.

"General Trang, I am your appointed liaison with

Hanoi in the administration of this facility—at *all* levels. You shall not—''

Something seemed to explode in Trang's brain. All of the anger and fear that had been building up inside him since the intruder's attack suddenly burst to the surface.

His meaty left hand swooped up and grasped Vinh's throat. He pushed Vinh backward several feet until they reached Trang's desk and until the smaller man's back was bent across the desk top. Trang's furious grip held him down; the general's other hand held the pearl-handled knife. The blade was out and rested lightly across Nguyen Vinh's throat.

The general felt perspiration beads dripping from his own forehead, and he watched them splash down onto Vinh's worried face.

''I shall do exactly as I wish, comrade. You are an outsider here. You would do well to remember that. These guards are my men. This is my prison.''

Vinh made an effort not to let his panic show. But it was only that: an effort.

''General, please! Release me. . .you don't know what you're doing!''

Even as he heard his liaison man's words, Trang knew that the little weakling was right. He had lost his temper, plain and simple.

The commandant stood back from Vinh, releasing the smaller man. Trang's mind was already clicking, estimating the consequences of his unwise outburst. An idea came to him.

There was a way he could cover himself. . . .

"Perhaps you are right," he said to Vinh, with only a suggestion of contriteness. "But you are not a man who chooses his words wisely, comrade."

The Hanoi liaison straightened to his feet. He massaged his throat with a hand. He appeared loath to say anything that might set Trang off again. "What about the prisoner McFee?"

Trang folded and pocketed his knife as if nothing had happened.

"The prisoner is being well cared for until I have time to deal with him properly," the general said. "Our first priority now is to prepare this installation for an actual escape attempt.

"My guess is that the lone man this morning had no intention of rescuing McFee. He was merely conducting a reconnaissance probe, and luck went against him. His people must think that if they strike quickly, they will have a chance. But they will have *no* chance. And now, I will take my leave.

"You will wait here, Mr. Vinh. I am sure that Hanoi does not want their people exposed to hostile fire."

Trang did not wait for a response. He left the office. Vinh remained behind, as Trang knew he would.

The general walked away from the office toward the security station down the corridor, and felt his lips curl back with a satisfied smile.

He had not expected any real resistance to his suggestion that Vinh remain behind. The Hanoi liaison had little stomach for the realities that comprised General Trang's world.

Nor did Trang regret his outburst. He knew, however, that his intimidation of Vinh could be only temporary. He would have to move fast if he wanted to deal with Vinh before the little man reported Trang's insubordination to Hanoi. Which is why Trang hoped that the big American's rescue team would strike soon. The sooner the better.

Then Trang would deal with them, most certainly.

He would also deal with Nguyen Vinh.

The general did not underestimate the man from Hanoi. Vinh may have been a womanly coward, but he had a certain native intelligence and persistence. He was also annoyingly curious. And honest. Trang's reading was that Vinh would never even consider taking a bribe, as the liaison's two predecessors had. Vinh had spoken several times of his repulsion at the corruption that had been such a problem in the government since the war. Trang knew that this sense of morality made Vinh particularly dangerous.

Yes, Vinh had to be dealt with on a *permanent* basis before his morality and his curiosity took him any closer to the truth.

The truth was that General Le Duc Trang was the undisputed boss of all the drug trade in this area of the Red River Delta.

His duty as prison commandant was the perfect cover. Every day there were trucks departing the rear loading dock with boxes of uniforms supposedly processed through the prison laundry for the nearby army base.

In reality, the trucks made important off-base stops between picking up the dirty laundry from the base and delivering it to the prison. The truck drivers met with the locals who grew the poppies. Their next stop was the secret lab area beneath the grounds of the temple-prison, before the trucks again carried their cargo away from that loading dock. Then they would rendezvous with the people with whom General Trang had made contact during his years as a ranking military man in this area. This was Trang's link in the chain, and it paid him handsomely. And yes, the prison was the perfect cover. Most of the guards stationed under Trang were from the rural peasant class. They had been easy to buy. Though only a trusted few, such as Lieutenant Khanh, knew the details of Trang's operation, the general nonetheless had his own private army in the guard force stationed at the temple.

There was plenty for Nguyen Vinh to snoop out and report to Hanoi. Vinh had arrived at his new position at the prison only ten days earlier, and so far he had not gotten lucky. But Trang understood the law of averages. Vinh was bound to ferret out something if he continued prying. There was no recourse but to kill the man.

It had to be done in a way that would cast no suspicion whatever on the general's position and his performance of his duties at the prison, so vital to the success of his operation.

Trang strode briskly through the archway leading to the security post, to take personal charge of the deployment of troops being sent over as reinforcements from the army base.

Trang was curious how many men would comprise the attack force. Would they all be as capable and deadly as the Occidental who had already penetrated these grounds and slaughtered so many guards?

The man Trang had witnessed in action had been no mere foot soldier, of that he was positive. He had been a professional, yes. A specialist.

A killing machine.

Trang had been truly impressed, and he did not relish the idea of a return engagement. But when it came—as it surely must—yes, it would serve Trang's purpose. And he would no longer be bothered with the nagging questions about the attack at dawn—whether it was Laotian, Thai, or American in origin, or even a subversive act from within the country, using Western mercenaries. These questions were political, entirely irrelevant to his personal "export operation."

All he cared about was that Nguyen Vinh would soon be an unfortunate sideline casualty—courtesy of General Trang, personally.

Vinh would be out of his hair for good.

And the big warrior of this morning could take the blame.

14

Bolan emerged from the waters of the Sông Hong several hundred yards upriver from the point where he had parted company from the Meos. If the Viets had been in hot pursuit when he hit that opposite shore, Bolan would not have wanted to draw them into the immediate vicinity of the guerrilla group.

The precaution of swimming against the current proved unnecessary, however. The army base downriver was late with their aerial support. Two Soviet-made M15 choppers came cranking in from the direction of the airstrip just as Bolan left the river waters and gained the bank.

The choppers did not pose an immediate threat. They were beginning their airborne search with a sweep downriver away from Bolan.

He moved quickly. He made the tree line of the jungle and hurriedly suited up. He had to locate Sioung and the group. Things would have to move very quickly now.

There was no sign of the Meos.

Despite the early hour, light sampan traffic was already beginning on the river. But Bolan had made it across without being seen, by swimming deep and conserving his breath with long, powerful strokes.

The sun had lost some of its bloodred intensity as it climbed higher into the eastern sky. The temperature was climbing too.

Bolan leathered the .44 AutoMag back in place. He palmed the silenced Beretta and cut deeper into the jungle. Some ten yards into the dense forest, he cut northward and began moving at a trot parallel to the riverbank but obscured from it by the thickness of the foliage. He was hoping the Meos had fallen back into this part of the jungle at the signs of trouble from the temple.

He came upon a deeply rutted gravel road. A vehicle was approaching from around a bend a half-kilometer away.

Bolan leaped behind a tree for cover. He brought up the Beretta. The vehicle, a vintage French colonial Citroën, pulled slowly into view. The Citroën had not aged gracefully. Few cars did in this humid corner of the world. But this rust-bucket seemed plagued by engine trouble, too.

The big man in black clearly heard tappets clattering under the hood as the car drew abreast of him. He saw through the windshield that the driver was concentrating intently on steering the Citroën around the deep ruts in the road.

When Bolan saw who the driver and passenger were, he stepped out from concealment while there was still time to flag the vehicle down.

The lovely Meo lady behind the wheel slowed the car to a stop. Tran Le's face lit up with relief. Beside her, her father also seemed happy to see Bolan. Sioung reached back and unlatched the rear door for the big American as Bolan approached, holstering his Beretta.

Bolan slid in behind the tribal headman and his daughter as Tran Le steered the heap around in a rough U-turn and drove back the way they had come.

"Thanks for the pickup," said Bolan with sincerity. "Your timing can't be beat. Where did the car come from?"

Sioung half turned in the front seat.

"Car belongs to Communist Party member who lives nearby," he replied. "Very few have cars in this area, even like this one. But it will do, I think."

"And the party member?" asked Bolan.

Sioung's daughter responded to that. She had caught Bolan's eye in the rearview mirror.

"This car was needed," she said quietly. "The party member was not. The car will not be missed or reported for hours. By then we will be gone."

The car emerged casually enough from the rutted road onto a secondary dirt road. Tran Le steered to the right on a northwesterly course. Bolan estimated that they were traveling roughly parallel with the Sông Hong, tracking upriver.

Low overhead, the two army choppers swooped by noisily. But Bolan had been absorbed into the ordinary scene that was whizzing by below the helicopters. The aged car did not arouse their suspicion. The choppers continued on a westward sweep.

That was one of the aspects of the war here that had been so infuriating, Bolan recalled: American forces had not been engaging a traditional military enemy at all. The Viet Cong had possessed the ability to utilize the landscape as an ally. They had been able to blend into its fabric, chameleonlike, and pop back out again at a moment's notice.

Exactly as Bolan was doing now.

Sioung, like the American and his daughter, watched the army helicopters *whump-whump*ing off into the distance. Then he turned to look back at Bolan.

"The gods smile upon you in your escape, Colonel Phoenix."

Tran Le nodded. "We were watching you from over here. When my father saw what was happening, he sent Krah Dac and me after this car we'd seen. We hoped you would be swimming on a downriver course to elude your pursuers. We were lucky to intercept you."

"Where are the others?" asked Bolan.

"I sent the others upriver one kilometer," replied Sioung. "They took the equipment you left behind with ours. We go there now."

"What of Colonel McFee?" asked Tran Le.

Bolan grunted.

"He's the only one who wasn't lucky this morning. Trang has to be on the ball enough to realize we wouldn't try a one-man bust-out operation after McFee. He's probably already pieced together that what just happened was a soft recon probe that went sour. He's probably tightening and beefing up his security right now. That's going to make busting McFee out of that place a whole lot tougher."

Sioung's dark eyes burned fiercely.

"Meo fear nothing, Colonel. We are ready to back you."

"Deo Roi and the others will be ready to move out as soon as we rendezvous with them," added Tran Le.

"Good," approved Bolan. He wanted to ask Tran Le if she had spoken to Deo Roi about the rivalry the young buck was brewing up between himself and Bolan. But he decided not to mention it in front of Sioung. Tran Le's father had enough on his mind. Bolan stuck to business. "Our only chance—McFee's only chance—is to hit them *now* as fast as we can before Trang has a chance to set up his security as strongly as he'd like. I'll radio in for air support and the pickup as soon as I get back to my equipment."

Through the car window off to their right, past occasional breaks in the jungle, Bolan could see glimpses of the Sông Hong as their course took them through rural countryside on a track that seemed to be drawing closer to the river.

The Citroën passed occasional thatched huts along the road. Bolan could see smoke rising from the chimneys as the women prepared breakfasts of rice and vegetables before leaving with their men to work in the rice paddies.

At one point, Tran Le had to brake to a halt while three young boys herded a half-dozen water buffalo across the road.

When they were moving again, Sioung spoke in a voice so mellow it surprised Bolan.

"The pace of life goes on," said the headman, inspecting the scene passing beyond the windshield. "It makes me think of better times. When my country was all like this. For everyone—Montagnard and Viet. But that was long ago. My wife—Ti Bahn—and I, we were young. We did not understand how soon peace would end, never to return."

His daughter reached across and touched a delicate hand to the headman's shoulder.

"Please, my father. You must concentrate on what we have to do. Things will happen very quickly now. Your mind must be clear for the fighting ahead."

Tran Le was a most singular female, for sure. As beautiful as she was deadly. As tough as she was exquisite.

Sioung reacted to the woman's show of strength. He sat more upright in his seat, recharged with the fortitude and bearing that were his natural style.

"You are right as usual, my daughter. Sometimes I think I am past my best years. I many times think of the past more than the present. But I have seen so much. It is now two years since your mother died, fighting at my side. Two years. But the ache only grows worse as the years pass. I miss Ti Bahn so much...."

The older man's voice sounded weary beyond description. All three in the car lapsed into silence.

Bolan briefly considered the conversation. He understood what Sioung was talking about. The bottom line was that this operation concerned far more than rescuing one American trapped inside that temple-prison on the Sông Hong. That was the top priority at this point, sure. But the big picture was that in some way this would be a step closer toward restoring a semblance of personal freedom and human dignity to these people—basic rights that had been lost, been trampled, beneath the present regime.

Most Americans had apparently forgotten America's commitment to bring freedom to the people in this area of the world.

Bob McFee had not forgotten, however.

And neither had Mack Bolan.

Bolan—Sergeant Mercy, Mack the Bastard—always figured that these proud human beings and this land of simple beauty were worth the commitment.

Another five minutes, and Tran Le swung the Citroën off the road onto another narrow, deeply rutted car path that led back into the dense jungle.

The little car bounced along the bumpy road. The lush green vegetation closed in around them as they left all signs of civilization behind. But the aged Citroën pushed on.

A slow half-kilometer farther, and the jungle gave way to a small clearing that was another of the many coves carved by nature into the shoreline of the Sông Hong.

Deo Roi and the other two surviving warriors of the Meo group stood waiting here. Near them was a camouflaged tarp-covered clump just short of the tree line, which must have been the weapons and equipment for this operation, including Bolan's. Two sampans had also been pulled ashore and stashed beneath the heavy jungle undergrowth.

Tran Le came to a stop several feet short of the clearing. Bolan and the two Meos got out. The waiting warriors stepped forward in greeting.

Outwardly, the men appeared calm. Krah Dac and Y Bo puffed on pipes of foul-smelling tobacco, which, Bolan recalled, the tribe grew and cured in their homeland mountains. But he also sensed a heavy expectancy in the air.

Bolan looked toward the river, getting his bearings. Tran Le had driven them in a wide diversionary circle to this new location, which offered a view of the temple-prison from across a somewhat wider expanse of water than before.

The coolness of dawn had dissipated into the muggy heat of the tropics. The Sông Hong had become host to a steady flow of river traffic. The workday had begun.

And across the river, General Trang would be tightening his security like a fist. Going hard all the way. The guy had every right to feel confident of smashing this escape attempt.

But Bolan still had an ace up his sleeve. Jack Grimaldi.

Deo Roi and the two other warriors reached the car. There was a brief staccato exchange in Meo. Bolan understood enough of the dialect to ascertain that Sioung was giving his men a quick rundown on what they had missed downriver.

Bolan slipped away from the group while the conversation was in progress. He crossed to the tarp-covered equipment near the tree line. He pulled back the camouflage and quickly located his own gear and AKM.

Bolan slung the AKM over his shoulder. He stooped and made a quick inventory of his equipment.

He knew immediately that something was missing.

A vital something.

Bolan's communication link with Grimaldi was the small high-powered transmitter, about the size of a belt ammo pack, that was equipped with a high-speed scrambler precoded to shoot one brief programmed message to summon Grimaldi from the base by the Thai-Laotian border.

The transmitter was missing.

Mack Bolan was deep inside Vietnam, and he had just lost all contact with the outside world.

15

Tran Le could not get her mind, or her eyes, from the powerful figure of Colonel John Phoenix.

She stood near her father, as a dutiful daughter should, listening to Sioung describe briefly the withdrawal of Colonel Phoenix from the temple-prison.

But Tran Le could not stop her attention from wandering when she saw the tall figure in combat garb discreetly break from the group without much notice from the others.

Tran Le alone watched as Colonel Phoenix walked to the equipment that Deo Roi and the other warriors had carried here from downriver.

The American moved with an animallike economy of movement that radiated male power and confidence.

Tran Le was surprised at herself despite the tension of these final brief moments before the group made its strike on the prison.

She would kill or be killed during the next hour.

She felt pangs of worry for her father. What was this talk in the car of his having passed his best years?

The question and concern nagged at her, refusing to let go.

And yet amid all of it, here she was feeling a strong attraction to a foreigner who had come to help them.

But he *was* worth responding to, she thought to herself. Okay, in some ways the big, strong, silent American was the very embodiment of the romantic American image. But Tran Le also sensed a warm, full soul of humanity that was equally a part of his aura. There was a gentleness about Colonel Phoenix. The kind of gentleness and warmth that was all too rare in the world of hatred and death that was her day-to-day reality.

Any woman would look twice at a male such as Colonel Phoenix, Tran Le reasoned to herself. A healthy woman of any race could not help but wonder what it would be like to be loved physically by this man....

She continued to watch him as he threw back the tarp from the stack of equipment. She was no longer even half listening to her father and his men.

Tran Le saw Colonel Phoenix retrieve his rifle and gear. She saw him make a quick check of it. And she saw the manner in which he looked up from that gear. He was gazing around the area near the pack, as if for indications of something.

Tran Le stepped away from the group of tribesmen. She walked toward the American as he was covering the other equipment with the camouflage.

"Colonel Phoenix?"

"Yes, Tran Le." He swung around when he heard her approach. His greeting was friendly enough. But Tran Le felt self-conscious before the gaze of those deep blue eyes.

"I—I saw you standing over here," she said in a voice she barely recognized as her own. "You appeared. . .concerned about something. Is everything all right?"

"I had a transmitter with my equipment. It's missing. I was about to look for it."

"I want to help," Tran Le said promptly. "Do you have any idea who may have taken it?"

The big American's face seemed to flicker for a moment with his decision on how much to divulge.

After a pause he said, "That can wait. The important thing now is to find that transmitter. Then I can pull in some air cover to get McFee out of here. It's more important than ever now. Trang is bound to have a hot reception waiting for us."

"Whoever it was who took your radio must have done it while Deo Roi and the other two were bringing the equipment upriver," Tran Le thought out loud.

Bolan nodded.

"You've got it. And they could only have arrived here a few minutes ago. The guilty one hasn't had much time to get rid of the transmitter, or he would have been missed. I doubt if he's carrying it, so unless he pitched it into the water—which would also attract the others' attention—then he must have thrown it away somewhere right around here. Tran Le, if you take the area to the left of us, I'll cover the ground to the right."

They split up. She glanced over at the men grouped near the car. The conversation appeared to have become a heated debate, mostly between Tran Le's father and Deo Roi. No one over in that direction seemed to be paying any attention to her or the American.

Except for once, when Deo Roi saw her away from the group. He threw her a long look that she felt even from that distance. But he was engrossed in the conversation with Sioung.

Tran Le could not hear their words. She was sure that they concerned Colonel John Phoenix. Deo Roi seemed obsessed with Colonel Phoenix and why he was here. But Tran Le thought she knew the reason why.

She had certainly not been oblivious to the naked lust that had always been in Deo Roi's eyes whenever he looked upon her. But she had had no sexual contact with him. She knew he resented this. It was this same emotional reasoning that now clouded Deo Roi's mind with resentment against the American.

Tran Le had covered some ten square yards of jungle foliage when she found the transmitter.

"Colonel Phoenix," she whispered. "Over here."

She pitched her voice low enough so it could not be overheard by her father and the others. For she had seen something alongside the transmitter....

She watched the big American move effortlessly toward her through the thick jungle growth. Then he was beside her. He stood looking down at where the missing transmitter lay tangled in a vine on the ground.

The transmitter was a ruined mess. Someone had dropped it here and stomped on it with a heavy boot. Amid the shattered casing the transistorized guts sparkled in the morning sunlight.

The American did not register any of the disappointment that Tran Le was certain he must have felt. His attention focused on what else Tran Le had seen.

There were footprints in the peat, which was still damp from the morning dew: the clearly outlined indentation of a boot sole, the patterned imprint pointing away from the sabotaged transmitter, in the direction of the cove clearing.

Tran Le recognized that boot print.

The American continued to be as perceptive as Tran Le guessed him to be. He eyed her again with a steady gaze.

"Do you recognize that boot print, Tran Le?"

"Yes. . . the pattern, the chipped heel, it belongs to Deo Roi."

Tran Le's reply was automatic. But within her she immediately questioned if she had done the right thing, passing this information on to the foreigner. It was, after all, a Meo matter. Deo Roi was at least right about that much.

But Tran Le felt an even stronger responsibility to this mission. The best interests of the mission would not be served by lying to a good man who had come halfway around the world to help her people.

Colonel Phoenix did not register surprise at her identification of the footprint. Tran Le knew that her information only confirmed a suspicion the fighting man had already entertained.

His blue eyes were icing over again. Tran Le felt a quiver course through her body.

"We don't have time to sit around and sort this thing out now," he said, the chilled steel back in his voice again. "It's time to lay out our plan of attack and proceed with it."

"And Deo Roi?"

"Yeah," said Colonel John Phoenix. "It's time to deal with Deo Roi too."

He started back toward the clearing. Toward Tran Le's father. Toward Deo Roi himself and the other two warriors. Proud Meo warriors who might not take well to the things that Tran Le had told this stranger.

She hurried along after him.

She found herself giving one final fleeting thought to what might have been. How nice if she had met this strong, gentle giant some other time under different circumstances. How *fine* they would have been together.

But this was a war zone, a new war zone, and a heated battle was about to commence. The odds against their little group were growing all the time. The loss of the American's transmitter made things desperate.

It would have been nice indeed to have met this colonel other than here. And perhaps, if things did go well, there would still be time to probe the soul of a man so possessed of the spirit of the Meo. Time to see if the attraction was mutual. And perhaps to act on it. . . .

Tran Le's mind came back to the present. The knowledge that she might very well cease to exist before the morning was over brought a crisp objectivity to everything around her.

Including Colonel Phoenix. She simply could not stop thinking about the man.

He was a magnificent specimen. And an unpredictable one. In a most dangerous, unpredictable situation.

What would he do next?

16

The Meo team formed a loose circle around Bolan as he knelt and used a twig to draw a rough map of the temple-prison in the sand of the cove's narrow beach.

The Executioner was experiencing all manner of memory flashes from his previous tours of duty in these jungles. It occurred to him how similar was this last-minute briefing with the Meos to the old days of Able Team.

General Trang's prison across the Sông Hong: the objective waiting to be hit.

And the last-minute rundown on the strategy that Bolan had been devising ever since Sioung and Tran Le picked him up after the probe.

The atmosphere was the same—the humidity already heavy; the jungle all around a moist, living, *breathing* thing that could turn against you all on its own.

And yeah, the presence of death that touched all the people here, sobering them all with its nearness.

Déjà vu for sure.

There was one difference.

The woman, Tran Le.

Though he was occupied with other priorities, Mack Bolan was by no means oblivious to the womanness of the beautiful, delicately boned Asian. It was too damn bad that he and Tran Le had not met under other, saner circumstances.

There were unmistakable vibrations between himself and this fine woman that could have led to their sharing a most interesting private space. *If* the circumstances had been right.

But the circumstances most assuredly were not right. Bolan thought no more about it.

The plans for the escape attempt had to be modified, of course, now that there would be no Jack Grimaldi. The original plan had called for the flying ace to give Bolan and company some air support and then lift McFee and Bolan out of the action to safety while the Meos covered their withdrawal.

The basic objective still held: get Bob McFee out of that prison. Getting Bolan and McFee back to the States, however, was a bridge that would have to be crossed when there was more breathing time to think about it.

Bolan pointed to his diagram in the sand as he spoke to the Meos.

"There's a loading dock that stretches out from the back of the temple," he told them. "It can't be seen from the river, otherwise it would blow the cover that the temple isn't just a temple. And I know for a fact that more than prison laundry is leaving that dock. I think General Trang is very sensitive to the area back there."

"Drugs," nodded Sioung from where he stood.

Bolan glanced at him.

"Heroin. How did you guess?"

Tran Le replied: "It would be unusual for a man of power at General Trang's level not to be involved in the drug trade. Even the Meo people have at times been drawn into it."

"I hear it said that one man controls all the drug trade in this area," said Sioung. "Perhaps the general is powerful enough to be that man."

"Could be. He's not running a small operation, that's for sure," Bolan said. "So, we concentrate our attack on the loading area to the rear. That will be Trang's weak spot if he does have anything stored there. It will be free of 'official' protection.

"Deo Roi, I want you, Krah Dac and Y Bo to cross the river and spread yourselves out along the jungle line facing the loading dock. Open fire and pour everything you have into that sector.

"Trang is expecting us to make a hit. All right, we'll make him think that the whole thing is coming down from his rear flank. He'll buy that, especially if he's jumpy about his drug operation. That will be our diversion. My guess is that he'll start pulling men from other positions and funnel them back there as soon as the shooting starts.

"Tran Le, you'll cross the river with your father

and me. I'm sure Trang is beefing up his guard force with men from that army base. He'll probably station guards along the line of pagodas between the river and the temple. You must give your father and myself the covering fire we need while we negotiate that chain-link fence and approach the main building.

"Sioung, you and I are going to run into heavy resistance from the guards along that stretch. But hopefully some of them will be the men Trang pulls around back when he thinks the loading dock is under fire.

"Once we reach the end of the building where McFee is being held, I'll plant the satchel explosive and blow the wall out. We grab McFee and git."

Sioung spoke again. "And if Trang has moved the prisoner?"

"A very real possibility," admitted Bolan. "In this case, we *find* the prisoner—then get out. I think we stand a good chance of making it if Tran Le keeps giving us heavy fire cover and Deo Roi and his men keep the diversion going."

Deo Roi finally spoke. He obviously wished to force an issue. "And what of the air support you promised, Colonel Phoenix?"

"It looks like there won't be any air support," Bolan said. "Someone here knows why."

Deo Roi did not respond directly. "It is an omen," he pronounced instead. "Only five Meo remain of our group—and this American will lead the rest of us to our deaths today. Can our cause afford this loss? This American's mission is not important enough to waste the life of the Meo!"

Krah Dac stepped forward before the American could respond. "I saw Colonel Phoenix fight on the river. He is as brave and strong as any Meo."

Tran Le also spoke in Bolan's defense. "You forget, Deo Roi. The American prisoner, McFee, is important to our cause as well."

The young buck waved her objection aside. "The two Americans will leave us behind to killing and more slaughter while they fly away to their comfortable lives in the West!"

Sioung glared sternly at the younger Meo. The headman's tone was severely reprimanding. "Would you go with them if you could, Deo Roi? Or would you stay behind with the rest of us and honor that which we have promised to do, even if you are asked to risk your life?"

Deo Roi bristled. "You make it sound as if I am a coward when you know this is not so, my respected leader. I have the interests of the Meo in my heart!"

Bolan chose that moment to interrupt.

"Sioung, we must move with all due haste. Trang will be moving quickly if he expects an attack."

Sioung nodded. "Colonel Phoenix is right." He shifted his attention from Deo Roi to include the others in his group. He spoke in a voice that showed he was used to being obeyed. "Arm yourselves. Prepare to cross the river. Are there questions?"

There were none.

The Montagnards broke the huddle and began moving toward their equipment.

"Deo Roi. Wait. You and I must speak," Bolan called out quietly.

Sioung and his people continued on out of earshot as if by common agreement. Deo Roi turned and retraced his steps to face Bolan.

The Meo warrior's broad shoulders were bunched up tightly, as were his facial muscles. It was clear he was not going to step back from any confrontation with Bolan.

"Yes, American? What is it?" Deo Roi's voice was a low, angry snarl. "Say your last words before you lead more of my people to their deaths."

"No one will die if we keep coolheaded and work with each other," Bolan replied evenly. "You're acting like a damn kid, Deo Roi. It is *your* attitude that will cost our side lives."

The Meo's hand went reflexively for the handle of a hunting knife sheathed at his belt.

"You dare to call me a child—"

Bolan was close enough to reach out and grab the man's wrist in a viselike grip, before the Meo had time to draw the knife even a fraction of an inch.

"Stop and listen to me, damn you!" growled Bolan. "You destroyed my communications link with the air cover. That could be a capital offense for you, Deo Roi—right here and now, in your own people's court. You aren't the first man to lose it over a beautiful woman. But I'm warning you, *knock it off*, my warrior friend. We need you, we need your spirit and capabilities. I'll forget about the transmitter. And you forget about Tran Le for the time being. We're both men. Let's be honest with each other, let us speak of our differences.''

The moment held. The line between pressure and explosion was stretched to the breaking point.

But something in Deo Roi, after these seconds of hesitation, responded to Bolan's words.

The Meo relaxed his posture.

Bolan warily released his grip on Deo Roi's wrist and stepped back. Deo Roi also backed up a pace away from Bolan.

''You are wise, American. What else do you know?''

''I know that you had better straighten this out in your mind before it gets you killed.''

The Meo glared hotly. ''I have a strong feeling for Tran Le. Yet she does not accept me as man. Am I not a man?''

''Perhaps she sees something lacking.''

The Meo responded to Bolan as if to a challenge. ''I? A Meo warrior! I lack *nothing* as a man.''

Bolan kept his voice at an even pitch. ''You lack the ability to hold your emotions in check at crucial times,'' he told Deo Roi. ''Sure, a man has to be in touch with what is in his heart and soul. He must follow those things. But there are times when other things are more important—such as survival. A man must learn to hide those feelings at times when he is required to go out and meet the world on its own terms. Do you understand what I say, Deo Roi? Do you understand the difference?''

Deo Roi's only response was a change of subject. "I go now to join my men," he said tonelessly. "If our talk is over."

"It's over. Good luck, Deo Roi."

The warrior's opaque eyes studied Bolan for another long moment, with a look that Bolan could not read.

"Good luck to you also, American," the tribesman said finally, in that same toneless voice.

Then Deo Roi turned to walk away toward the grcuping of his people around the equipment, where they were arming themselves and making the final preparations for the trip across the river.

Bolan ran through a last-minute inspection of his own weapons. The AKM, the Beretta Belle, Big Thunder were all ready for combat.

Bolan then joined the Meos for a final synchronization of timepieces and a run-through of the positions they would take once the strike commenced.

Time: 0628 hours.

Three hours since Grimaldi had air-dropped him into the jungle.

And the bottom line—the deadly bottom line—of

the Executioner's mission to Vietnam had been reached.

The strike to bust Colonel Bob McFee out of General Trang's maximum-security prison was on.

17

This time Bolan did not need the Starlight to make a visual sweep of the area before penetrating the prison grounds. A quick pan with the naked eye was enough to reveal the formidable odds that faced Bolan and his group.

The Executioner was once again in a prone position on the sloping bank of the Sông Hong. Ninety yards separated him from the chain-link fence that ran the perimeter of the temple grounds. He was approximately one kilometer upriver from his line of approach earlier that morning.

Beyond the fence the land sloped toward the wing of the "temple" where Mack Bolan had last seen Bob McFee. The last three of the string of pagodas stood between Bolan and his objective.

There were two distinct differences about advancing from this new direction. Like the pagodas he had encountered out front earlier that morning, these were mounted with rotating closed-circuit TV cameras. But this time men inside the security station would have their eyes glued to the monitor screens, watching intently for any sign of activity. And there were no shrubs and trees for Bolan to play as there had been out front.

Also, two uniformed Viet regulars armed with AK-47s had been posted between each of the pagodas.

There was now a steady flow of river traffic along the Sông Hong behind them. Bolan, Sioung, and Tran Le had blended in on their crossing, as had Deo Roi, Krah Dac, and Y Bo in the other sampan one-half kilometer upriver. The group had made its crossing undetected.

Of the guards at the two pagodas nearest to Bolan, two men were indulging in a smoke, and all were conversing across the hundred-yard distance that separated the pagoda structures from each other.

Bolan was alone now.

Sioung and Tran Le had moved off farther upriver, away from him.

Sioung was to position his daughter at the best spot strategically from which she could supply Sioung and Bolan with cover fire as they made their run for the main building.

At this moment, Deo Roi and the others were moving into location on the far side of the temple wing that served as the prison administration sector.

Within sixty seconds, the three Meo warriors would open fire with their Chinese Type 56 assault rifles, pouring all the firepower they could muster into General Trang's sensitive loading-dock area.

Sixty seconds beyond that, Bolan and Sioung would negotiate the chain-link fence and make their approach toward the corner of the prison wing facing them.

Bolan was fully equipped for the hard hit.

He had shed the all-purpose pouch and other unnecessary weight. All the munitions he would need were strapped to the military web belt around his waist, including the packet of plastic explosive that would give them access to the torture room where they hoped to find McFee.

It was 0650 hours.

Behind Bolan, the boat traffic, piloted by Vietnamese in black pajamas and broad-brimmed straw hats, seemed to continue as if by rote. No one traveling by took any notice of the figures moving about along the riverbank. Or at least no one raised an alarm.

Bolan heard footfalls.

Tran Le emerged from around a curve in the riverbank. The Asian beauty approached Bolan in a lithe crouch. She carried a heavy Type 56 that didn't seem at all out of place in her hands.

Bolan frowned. He had expected Sioung.

Tran Le avoided his gaze. She moved into a prone position alongside Bolan and peered over the rise with him in the direction of the pagodas and the men who stood guard there.

"It will begin at any second," she said.

There was steel in her voice.

But Bolan was not to be sidetracked.

"Where is your father?" he demanded.

The Meo woman continued to gaze straight ahead at the terrain before them as she replied.

"He will give us the covering fire."

"That was your job."

"I convinced my father that it would be better if he and I were to change places in your plan." Those warm brown eyes at last swung around to make contact. "I have been concerned about my father since he began talking about my mother in the car, do you remember? I have suggested to my father that he consider turning over command of our group to one of the younger men and continuing on in an advisory capacity, at least for a while. My father often seeks my counsel. I hope he follows it now. He and my mother were very close.

"It is the custom for Meo men to take several wives. We are a polygamous society. Yet my father took only my mother and lived with her for thirty years. She bore him eight children, and she was still fighting by his side until the time of her death two years ago. My father is one of the strongest men I have ever known. But the loss of my mother seems to be returning to haunt him. I do not want him where the fighting is heaviest, Colonel Phoenix.".

Inescapably Bolan's kind of woman.

He wondered briefly if Tran Le herself might be among those considered to head up the Meo unit....

Before he could put words to thought, a barrage of automatic-weapons fire opened up from the other side of the temple structure.

The steady clatter of Type 56s on full automatic mode was punctuated by the heavier booming of an RPG-7 grenade launcher and the subsequent, even louder, explosions of the hits.

Deo Roi and his men had launched their attack on the prison loading dock.

Bolan and Tran Le both swung their weapons up close to their bodies. They tensed for the assault.

"You have time to stay behind and give me cover fire," Bolan told her in the last seconds before combat. "It's going to be very hot from here on out."

Tran Le did not bat an eye.

"I am a Meo warrior, Colonel Phoenix. I have killed forty-one men during my time with this unit. I am ready to kill more."

The crackle of weapons fire from the jungle perimeter fronting the loading area—the "attack" of Deo Roi and his men—was now answered by smaller arms fire from what was most likely the dock area.

Bolan estimated that Trang would immediately start reinforcing his manpower at the hot contact point. And sure enough, within thirty seconds Bolan could see that some of the soldiers at the pagodas farther down the line, toward the front of the temple, were now thinning out to one man for each structure as half the force was ordered back into the main building.

The guards at the three pagodas nearest to Bolan remained at two men each, however. Trang apparently wanted security kept hard at this end of the administration wing. Bolan hoped that meant something.

Alongside him, Tran Le chuckled without humor as the sounds of battle continued.

"I guess this ends the general's use of the temple as camouflage for his prison," she said.

At that moment, heavy automatic-weapons fire opened up from Sioung's position upriver, around the big curve. The tribal chief was pouring it on hot and heavy. His brutal hail of 7.62mm projectiles delivered hellfire and death to the guards stationed beside the pagoda to Bolan's left.

Bolan was peripherally aware of twisting, stumbling bodies over there. He nudged Tran Le.

"This is it," he growled. "Let's move!"

Mack Bolan and Tran Le stormed over the embankment of the Sông Hong toward the chain-link fence.

Man and woman, side by side.

Into the fray.

Even before they hit the fence, Bolan was laying in a steady figure-eight of slugs from his AKM at the two soldiers by the pagoda along their right flank.

Beside him, Tran Le went about shorting out the fence.

The two guards careened back into their pagoda under the impact of the AKM slugs, the hits splashing a very ancient edifice with very contemporary blood.

Before the dead men had fallen, Tran Le had already negotiated the fence.

The three sentries from the next pagodas down the line were hustling in their direction. But Bolan gauged his numbers and made it over the fence before dealing with them.

The approaching guards opened fire from downrange. Several rounds banged in the early morning air. But the rounds went high.

The American man and the Asian woman, two well-tuned combat machines, made the run between two of the pagodas and on toward the temple, returning the guards' fire with short bursts before the Viets could adjust their aim.

One of the soldiers fell as if tripped by some invisible wire at ankle level. The other two fell away, each behind a different pagoda.

Bolan and Tran Le reached the end of the wing where Bolan had last seen Bob McFee. Their position was now exposed to both pagodas.

God knows what the people on the river thought was going down here.

The soldiers behind the pagodas opened fire with sporadic single shots, apparently going for increased accuracy. But the sight of their dead comrades must have been still fresh in their minds, for the shots were still too hastily triggered, missing high and chipping away at the face of the temple. But it could only be a matter of seconds before the soldiers finally corrected their aim. . . .

Bolan reached for the container of plastic explosive and fuse that rode his belt. He handed it to Tran Le even as his attention swung toward those guards firing down on them.

"Here, plant it at that wall," he said, nodding curtly toward where he wanted into the building.

Then Bolan dealt with those soldiers. He swung the AKM over his shoulder by its strap. He yanked one of the M34 incendiary grenades from his belt. He tugged the pin and hurled the HE at the pagoda to his right. The grenade had a four- to five-second fuse.

During those four to five seconds, two things happened.

The first was that Tran Le finished setting the plastic explosive where Bolan had indicated.

"Okay, set a ten-second fuse," Bolan ordered. "Then make tracks and hit the dirt!"

The second thing was that a silent, invisible object whipped by so close to Bolan's ear that he felt a hot-cold bite across the tip of his left earlobe. But it was fleeting, only a nick, and further sensation was submerged for now beneath the cold professional purpose that guided him.

He shielded his face with an arm and lowered his head.

The pagoda ahead erupted with an earthshaking flash of thunder. Mortar and brick sailed through the air. So did the guard who had been hiding behind the structure. What was left of him.

Bolan felt no compunction about leveling these an-

cient structures. It was not as if they were any longer
religious shrines. They had long ago been desecrated
by the men he now fought.

Mack Bolan had more respect than most for the
past. But he respected life even more. Especially, at
this moment, the life of Colonel Bob McFee.

Tran Le activated the plastic explosive's ten-
second fuse. Then she spun around from her work.
She and Bolan dashed away. The dust from the destroyed pagoda was still settling.

They both took a running dive and hit the turf like
two ball players making reckless headfirst attempts
to reach home plate.

The plastic explosive went off, blasting the base of
the temple structure, shaking the earth beneath them
again, raining on Bolan and the woman another
shower of mortar and dirt.

Bolan was the first to swing around into a prone
position. He sighted the soldier who had been firing
on them from behind the nearest remaining pagoda.
The guy hadn't spotted Bolan yet. The Viet was
holding his AK-47 at port arms, trying to see Bolan
and Tran Le through the settling dust of the two explosions. The guy was looking toward the area where
Bolan and the woman had just been. Not where they
were now.

Bolan triggered a single round that caught the
soldier high in the chest and took him out of commis-
sion permanently.

More guards were moving in from the pagodas farther down. Bolan judged them to be some two hundred or more yards away.

Now that the smoke had dissipated, a large, irregular hole gaped from what had been the corner of this wing of the "temple." From a distance, all Bolan could see inside was an unmoving, shadowy no-man's-land.

Without speaking, the American man and the Asian girl took back-to-back positions and went to work, squeezing off generally unaimed bursts at the troops advancing from down the line. Right away they scored a double-head hit.

Bolan could discern, behind the noise of his and Tran Le's weapons fire, the continuing sounds of battle issuing from the rear of the main building toward the loading-dock area. Deo Roi and his men were holding steady in their role as diversion.

Bolan headed for the hole in the wall.

Tran Le continued firing, no hits—the range was too great—but those soldiers went flying behind the cover of pagodas and returned only sporadic rounds, only too content to wait for reinforcements to back them up.

Bolan hit the hole in the wall and passed through with his AKM up and ready. With Tran Le's Type 56 stuttering steadily behind him, he gave General Trang's "interrogation room" a quick visual once-over.

There was no one to greet him.

No guards.

No prisoner.

Their luck had run out.

The wall shackles dangled empty where Bolan had seen the prisoner less than two hours ago.

The interrogation room was empty. All the way.

Yeah, Colonel McFee was gone.

18

Nguyen Vinh sat in the chair behind General Trang's desk. He was alone in the general's office. He was extremely uneasy.

The prison was under attack. The general had told him they were being hit at the loading area. The rattle of weapons fire from some distance beyond the walls of the office was steady in Vinh's ears. Occasionally he would hear the booms of heavier weapons and the sounds of explosions.

Vinh felt utterly helpless. He considered himself a man of letters, a man of breeding, intellect, peace. Yet he had a strong itch deep inside to be *doing something* at this moment.

Trang had manipulated him into staying behind, insisting that he did not want to risk the life of the party liaison. But Vinh was also a man whose skill at reading people had been honed to a fine art, the result of years of staying alive amidst the constant political infighting that was life in the nation's capital. Survival came from being able to assess and judge people accurately.

Vinh knew in his heart that Trang was up to no

good in this place. The government man had suspected it from his arrival ten days ago.

Vinh felt strongly that Trang was involved in something illegal. But thus far, he had been unable to unearth anything in the way of tangible evidence. The operation was too well-oiled, the men paid too well to keep their mouths shut.

An explosion that was louder—closer—than the others shattered his train of thought. The thundercrack rattled the very walls of the office, knocking several of the general's military citations and maps to the floor.

Nguyen Vinh sprang to his feet with impatience. He could sit still no longer. He wished more than ever that he carried a side arm. He started toward the door in a determined stride.

He knew where the armory was in the security station: he would arm himself immediately. A man of letters, of peace, yes. But a strong, determined man too. He could not sit idly by on the sidelines while others decided his fate.

Before Vinh reached the office door, however, it came flying open from a powerful kick from the outside corridor.

Vinh found himself standing face to face with a figure from hell.

The man was American. An imposing giant in full combat garb. An assault rifle hung by its strap over his left shoulder. His right arm was outstretched, and from it extended the largest handgun that Vinh had ever seen.

The man from hell took two steps into the office. The handgun tracked to a stop, drawing a bead on the space between Vinh's eyes from a distance of about five feet. Vinh felt perspiration gathering close to his hairline. He did not move.

"I want to know where the American McFee is," said the intruder in Vietnamese. Then in English: "Tell me where to find him. You have ten seconds to convince me that you know where he is and you're not lying. Begin now."

Vinh knew damn well how close he was to dying. This warrior giant had to be the same one that Trang had seen before. The enemy. One of those who had bombed Vietnamese cities.

Vinh sought to speak, but his voice was stuck in his throat.

Then he heard a faint whirring sound from somewhere in the office immediately behind him. The big American heard it, too. He looked over Vinh's shoulder.

Nguyen Vinh turned around to see what the noise was. There was a bookshelf built into one wall of the office. Or so it seemed. But that faint whirring was the sound of a hidden mechanism now sliding the bookshelf aside to reveal a hidden passageway. A stairway led down out of sight.

Vinh glanced back to the front door. The American had disappeared. But Vinh was certain the intruder had not gone far, that he was probably standing in the corridor just out of sight.

He returned his attention to the hidden passageway. General Trang emerged from it.

Vinh sensed something was terribly wrong here. Trang had not come to his rescue. Trang's manner indicated he was totally unaware of the confrontation that he had interrupted between Vinh and the American.

Of course! How foolish he had been! Trang was using this attack by the American and his forces as a cover to liquidate Vinh.

All this flashed through Vinh's mind with belated clarity at the instant that he saw what the general was doing with his right hand. Vinh recalled Trang once bragging about his Russian 9mm pistol. The general wore the Stetchin in a wooden holster. The holster doubled as a stock for the automatic pistol, which was how the general was now using it: he was holding the pistol in a firing position, aiming it directly at Vinh as he stepped into the room.

Trang snickered when he saw the expression on Vinh's face.

"Now you are out of my way forever, you troublesome—"

Vinh knew he was a dead men.

The man from hell stepped back into the office from behind the cover of the open door. The mighty hand weapon was extended at arm's length at the general.

"Your turn, General," the American said in English, softly.

Then the big man's hand cannon spoke with an ear-blasting report. A stab of saffron flame licked across the room before General Trang could bring his own weapon to life.

Death was in that room, yes. But not for Vinh. It was, as the American had said, the general's turn.

Trang caught the round between his eyes. The impact kicked what was left of him back through the hidden passageway and out of sight down the secret stairs with a loud clattering sound.

Vinh was dazed. He looked and saw the American appraising him. The hot handgun was held down at the man's side, harmless for a second. But Vinh knew that death was still in the room, waiting to reach out and touch him.

Vinh finally found his voice. "You...saved my life."

The American did not respond directly. Keeping an eye on Vinh, he crossed the office to look down the stairwell beyond the secret passage.

"Come here," he said to Vinh.

The little man was barely aware of the sounds of the continuing firefight from beyond the walls of the office as he moved to the man's side and followed the path of his eyes.

Vinh had not known that there was a level beneath the prison floor. It had a low ceiling, was well-lighted and modern. General Trang lay crumpled at the foot of the stairs. A murky puddle was spreading out on the shiny floor beneath his head. Beyond his body stretched what appeared to be a well-equipped laboratory.

"What is it?"

"A powder factory," the American told him. "For converting poppies into raw heroin."

Vinh turned to face the giant.

"Heroin?" he echoed. At most, he had suspected the general of running a black market operation.

"There's a major drug connection working out of this area," the American continued. "From what I see down there, I'd say the late general was that man."

"Wh-who are you?" Vinh inwardly cursed the quaver in his voice.

The American ignored the question.

"I saw you this morning when you and Trang were interrogating McFee," he said, looking back at Vinh with that death's-head stare. "Trang wanted to torture the prisoner. You tried to stop him. For that, you have a chance to live. *If* you help me."

Even in the heat of the moment, the man of peace within Nguyen Vinh felt an inner spasm of revulsion at making any sort of pact with this man of violence. This man from hell.

"But all of those soldiers you killed!" he could not help blurting out. "Men only doing their duty—"

"Criminals helping to channel powdered death around the world," countered the American. "Soldiers, yeah. But Trang couldn't have run this operation without having most of the staff on his own payroll. As for any soldiers who weren't working for Trang on the side—well, you people had no damn right to hold Bob McFee here in the first place," Bolan said with quiet force.

"Your only worry, if you do get out of here alive, is what your government will say to the world press about it. I'd whitewash it as a kickback from Trang's associates in the drug trade if I were you. But that's your problem. All I want now is McFee. Tell me where he is. You don't owe Trang a thing."

Vinh's mind had cleared. He found the objectivity to weigh what he had heard. The American was right. General Trang had represented all that Nguyen Vinh hated. Vinh's country could only call itself civilized once men like Trang had been routed from the people's government. He sincerely believed that.

And the humanity within Nguyen Vinh went out to the prisoner, McFee. The man had more than paid, whatever his sins against the Vietnamese people might have been.

Finally, Nguyen Vinh realized he owed his life to the big American warrior.

He made his decision.

"The general moved the prisoner to the prison holding cell," he told the infiltrator. "It is the first cell to your right along this corridor, beyond the guard station."

The fighting man nodded almost imperceptibly.

"Thank you. Now turn around, please. It will save you some explaining."

Vinh nodded. "I understand."

He turned his back to the man, knowing full well what was coming. The American was right: it would save explaining things to Hanoi.

As he stood facing the wall, he heard the sounds of the battle outside. He was thinking what a strange man the American was, a very special human being on many levels.

There was an abrupt burst of pain behind his left ear. Then he was swallowed up into the black void of unconsciousness.

Nguyen Vinh's last waking thoughts were: *I'm glad I have helped this American. Who could he be?*

19

Mack Bolan reached out and caught the falling form of the Viet VIP. Whoever he was, the man seemed to Bolan like a good person. In the wrong place at the wrong time.

Bolan eased the man's body to the floor of the office. He touched the man's pulse to ascertain if the Viet was okay. Satisfied, the Executioner turned and went back out to the corridor.

There was the chance, of course, that the VIP was sending him into the heat of action with false information. A wild-goose chase. But Bolan didn't read it that way. He felt confident he had gauged the man's responses accurately, that the Viet had told him the truth about the whereabouts of McFee.

The confrontation with General Trang and the civilian VIP had cost Bolan less than a minute in time lost.

The exchange of weapons fire continued unabated from the direction of the prison loading dock. Deo Roi and the other two Meo tribesmen still engaged General Trang's troops.

Tran Le came running down the corridor toward Bolan.

The Meo woman's high right cheekbone was smudged with gun oil. Her dark hair was wild and tangled. The Asiatic beauty of her face flushed with exertion.

She was, yeah, one beautiful woman. Especially at a moment like this.

"I took out the soldiers who were coming from in front." She looked through the open doorway of Trang's office at the crumpled form of the VIP. "Did you learn anything about McFee?"

"He's on the other side of the guard station," Bolan said. "And that means more guards," he added dryly.

Their eyes clashed.

"Do you try to frighten me?" she asked.

"Just warning you," he said, smiling in appreciation of her fine style. "Okay, let's move out. The security station is through that archway at the far end of the hallway. The hallway continues on the other side into the cellblock. That's where we find McFee."

They parted to opposite sides of the office corridor and advanced at a steady pace along the hallway toward the guard station.

"Why has no one from the guard station detected our approach?" Tran Le said in a hushed voice.

Bolan leathered his AutoMag and swung the AKM back around to firing position, flicking it into automatic mode.

"Trang was planning to kill one of his own people for personal reasons—he was going to use our hit as a cover and blame it on us," he replied. "Trang stationed his men outside, but he left this hallway clear of personnel so there wouldn't be any interruptions when he made his move. He could do that. He was the general."

Tran Le caught the key word.

"Was?" she echoed.

"You heard it right," Bolan grunted.

Then they hit the guard station.

Bolan went through the archway first. He exploded into the room. Tran Le was immediately behind him.

Two guards had their attention on the TV consoles linked to the pagodas out front. Another man held a walkie-talkie to his mouth while he stood in the archway that faced the loading area, watching the defensive line of men along the dock who were answering the fire of the Meos out in the jungle.

All three guards swung around at the commotion of Bolan's and Tran Le's entrance.

One guard never made it out of his chair at the console. The console was suddenly splashed with his blood and brains. One down.

The remaining two guards made a grab for their nearby AK-47s. But that was all they could do.

Bolan and Tran Le took out one each. The hammering of their weapons fire was near deafening in the close confines of the room. Two more bodies danced death jigs into eternity.

And the road to Bob McFee was open.

Hopefully.

But their trouble had in fact only just begun. Tran Le put it into words as she looked away from the carnage and down the corridor leading to the loading dock.

"They've heard us, Colonel. They're sending men this way."

As she spoke, the door leading outside to the front temple grounds swung open. Bolan remembered that the door was camouflaged into the face of the temple.

Sioung had discovered the doorway. The Meo headman had been toting his Type 56 at a run for some distance. He seemed somewhat winded, but his eyes were bright with the fire of battle, and his voice was steady as he entered the guard station and saw Bolan and his daughter.

"May Sioung be of assistance, Colonel? I waited at assigned post but soon killed all the soldiers who came near me."

"Always glad to see a friend," Bolan grinned. "So how about some firepower to keep those guys pinned down at the loading dock? I'm gonna grab McFee. Then we pull out through the front door and make a run for the river."

"It shall be done," said Sioung.

Sioung and Tran Le crossed briskly to the archway leading to the loading area. Several soldiers were advancing along the corridor toward the security station, drawn by the fire in there.

Father and daughter opened up, their assault rifles both on automatic mode. The Meos crouched low as they fired to avoid the answering rounds from the soldiers. Bullets chipped away slivers of door frame and whistled into the room. The Meos kept up a heavy, steady barrage down the corridor.

Bolan slammed through the door into the opposite wing of the "temple." The cellblock. Concrete walls extended down the full length of the building, with locked metal doors every ten feet breaking the monotony.

One guard was stationed midway down the cellblock. He moved into action, bringing his AK-47 around toward firing position. But not fast enough.

Bolan snapped off a short burst. The man died in a shimmering red mist of blood suddenly released from the veins and bone of his head.

Shouting erupted instantly from every cell along the wing. A weird echoing cacophony of foreign tongues, all pleading.

Bolan turned to the first door on the right. Behind it he was supposed to find Bob McFee. He prayed that the guy was there. And still alive. McFee had not looked any too well when Bolan had seen him earlier that morning.

Bolan again transferred weapons. The big stainless-steel AutoMag was back as head weapon. Bolan stood alongside the door and blew the lock to bits. Then he entered the room, low and fast.

The room was empty.

Except for Bob McFee.

The Viet vip had told Bolan that this was the temporary holding area for incoming prisoners. Trang apparently had still not wanted McFee mixed with his regular charges. So McFee was in here instead.

The prisoner was standing under his own strength. He was shackled at both wrists. Chains from the shackles were riveted into the brick wall. He looked worse than before. A flattened nose had been added to his injuries since Bolan had seen him last. McFee watched Bolan approach now, with spirited eyes that still sparkled behind bloated purple bruises.

"You were the one who raised all hell this morning, weren't you?" he croaked through the bloody remains of his lips. "I knew you'd make it back. You sure call 'em close, don'cha?"

The voice carried the fierce fire of life, weak as it was.

"Watch your hands, Bob," Bolan warned. "We're getting out of here."

Bolan triggered two rounds from the .44 at the shackle mountings. The chains snapped away from the wall, the manacles remaining around McFee's wrists but now useless to detain him.

"Can you make it out on your own feet?" Bolan asked.

McFee gave it a good try before responding. He took two halting steps. Then his knees buckled. With a groan he began to collapse.

Bolan moved forward quickly, offering support.

McFee's left arm wrapped around Bolan's shoulders. Bolan halted the drop, and at that moment the two men eyeballed each other from a distance of some six inches. But there was no recognition. McFee was a man only half alive, if that.

Bolan wanted to tell McFee just who it was that had "raised all hell." But he could not. Not now. There wasn't time.

"Hang tight," Bolan said. "We're going to make it out of here."

"I haven't a doubt in the world," McFee responded.

Bolan guided McFee's limp form out of the cell and back toward the security room.

Everyone in the cellblock was still shrieking as Bolan closed the door behind himself and McFee.

The fighting in the guardroom had subsided. Sioung and Tran Le were snapping off single shots down the corridor and were being answered in same. It was a temporary standoff.

Bolan also saw that the fighting in the loading area had stopped. Which meant that Deo Roi and his men had fallen back into the jungle. Having to search for McFee had taken up valuable time. Deo Roi and the other two Meos were pulling away as per schedule. Which meant that some of those troops who had been defending the dock area would now be free to leave that area and swing around to box in Bolan and his group from different angles.

"All right, out the doorway," he urged the others.

"Don't bunch up. Move away from the building and get to that damn river any way you can. But help each other. Let's do it!"

Sioung pushed out in the lead, through the doorway leading onto the acreage fronting the edifice. The headman's Type 56 was high and ready as he ran.

Bolan went next. The .44 swung in wide arcs from his right fist as he moved along at a brisk sprint, supporting Bob McFee with his left arm. The two Americans functioned as a smooth team.

Tran Le came last. Toting the eleven-pound weapon didn't slow down the slender woman at all.

As they ran into the hot Vietnamese sunshine, onto the sloping grounds that were dotted with pagodas, Bolan heard the man he was carrying grunt something into his ear.

"Give 'em hell, soldier," McFee exhorted.

Hell yeah, the Executioner was going for it in Vietnam.

One more time, yeah.

With everything he had.

20

At first the Bolan group met only light resistance in its withdrawal from the temple. Sioung had already shredded one man's stomach and crotch and sent two other green-uniformed Viet regulars scurrying for cover as Bolan, McFee, and Tran Le joined him on a gravel driveway.

The waters of the Sông Hong sparkled in the sunlight, separated from them by the three hundred sloping yards interrupted by the line of pagodas. River traffic had finally come to a standstill as the battle raged.

"Hold on, Bob," said Bolan. "We're going piggy-back."

Bolan stooped and hefted the battered POW in a standard fireman's carry over his back. The arm ending with the AutoMag was still free to track.

Bolan broke into a steady jog. He angled in a wide circle away from the pagoda where the two Viet guards had sought cover from Sioung's heavy fire.

From Sioung himself came a brisk order to Tran Le.

"My daughter, fall in with me behind the Americans' flank as we proceed. Quickly now!"

"Yes, father."

As he hustled along with Bob McFee over his back, Bolan heard the steady kill force of both assault rifles as father and daughter opened up with a barrage of fire to cover their retreat. He couldn't tell what hits were scored. He had to keep moving.

Answering fire flared up from behind them in the direction of the temple. Once again Mack Bolan heard the whistling sounds of death zipping all about him. He still had congealed blood on him from the last nick at his ear. Nasty. He continued to move low and fast in a zigzag pattern.

They had covered nearly half the distance to the river and were well past the line of pagodas when two separate occurrences caught Bolan's attention.

Deo Roi and the other two tribesmen of the Meo group—Krah Dac and Y Bo—suddenly came tearing in a mad dash toward Bolan and friends from around the end of the administration wing of the temple.

And a bulky Soviet MI5 chopper came sailing into the area from the direction of the army base one and a half kilometers away. The craft was equipped with a 12.7mm machine gun and four 57mm rocket pods.

The pilot did not seem interested in Deo Roi and the others running in from downrange. The MI5 zoomed in low out of the sun toward Bolan and his group.

The pilot triggered off one of the rocket pods at about two hundred yards out. With a strong *whoosh* the rocket tore along its one-second course in a tail of flame and smoke, exploding only short yards away from Bolan, McFee, and the father-and-daughter Meo team. A roar of smoke and flying dirt enveloped them.

Then the machine gun opened up, spitting lead as the chopper flew by low overhead.

Bolan dodged out of the way at the last minute, without dropping Bob McFee. A sizzling stream of slugs zipped up a line of tiny mud clods along the track where Bolan and McFee had been mere seconds ago.

Bolan heard a gasp of pain from Sioung's direction. He looked. The Montagnard tribal chief was lurching into a dizzy spin. Blood geysered from his left arm.

The Executioner returned his eyes to the chopper that had swooped by. The MI5 was circling, preparing for another run at the exposed group on the ground. And another run would be all it would take to finish them off. Unless the damn thing was stopped.

But the chopper *was* stopped, yeah.

Not by Bolan.

Before he could swing his AKM around for at least a shot at the death-dealing bird, a shrill screech filled the air.

A jet craft whistled in from the south, approaching at a near-impossible altitude of about sixty feet.

An AV-8B Advanced Harrier.

Grimaldi.

The Harrier was totally loaded for combat: two 30mm cannons and seven fully mounted store stations sprouting a variety of bombs, rocket pods, and AIM-9 missiles.

Grimaldi triggered a 30mm that pointed with a finger of tail smoke at the cockpit of the army chopper. The helicopter blossomed into a flower of red flame. It tumbled to earth with a loud metal-rending crash.

The Harrier screeched off into a wide, circling curve that was almost faster than the naked eye could follow. Two more rockets were fired as the VTOL craft jetted by again, with a tad less speed this time.

Uniformed troops from the direction of the temple had been advancing slowly after Bolan and his party. One of Grimaldi's rockets scored a nice hit amid a cluster of regulars. The ground shook, flame flared again as broken bodies were tossed into the air like discarded rag dolls seeping fluids from leaks and tears. The second HE scored a near miss. But it was enough to disperse those troops and all but halt any advance from that sector.

The Harrier banked into another curve that circled directly overhead above Bolan and McFee and the two Meos. It was great to see the VTOL in the hands of a friend, not an enemy as in Maryland during the Iranian hit team mission, when the plane was witness to a showdown scene of hemorrhaging enmity.

The state-of-the-art craft hovered for a few seconds like some noisy metal insect. Then the pilot activated the Harrier's vertical landing controls, and the jet began settling to earth for the pickup. The downward blast sent dirt and rocks flying.

Bolan glanced briefly at Tran Le and her father. Tran Le was helping Sioung to his feet, steadying him. The tribal headman gripped a bloody patch at his shoulder. The Montagnard's proud face quivered with what must have been incredible pain. But at least he was alive. Tran Le stepped away. Sioung stood and began moving under his own power again.

At that moment, Deo Roi, Krah Dac, and Y Bo came running up to Bolan and the others. Deo Roi approached Bolan and there was none of the earlier antagonism in the young warrior's eyes or manner as he spoke.

"Colonel, my men and I pulled out. But we saw no sign of you and others withdrawing. We came to help!"

He had to shout in Bolan's ear to be heard above the high keening whistle of the landing Harrier.

Bolan extended an arm and shook hands with this fearless soldier.

"You're a brave man, Deo Roi," he shouted back, still bearing the weight of McFee. "You did good work today. I'm taking this man out, and you've got enough breathing room now to withdraw. Take care with Sioung. He's wounded."

The Meo nodded briskly.

"It has been good to work with you, Colonel Phoenix. Good luck to you."

The Meo turned and moved off, without waiting for a response, to pass the word along and organize the pullout. Bolan had decided to bury the matter of the sabotaged transmitter for good. Deo Roi had more than redeemed himself during the hellfire of the past thirty minutes. The young man was all business as Bolan saw him issue orders to the others. Deo Roi had it in him to be one hell of a leader of men, Bolan knew that. And the guy had obviously wrestled his personal inner demons under control. They no longer undermined the work of a warrior. Deo Roi had become a man.

The Harrier touched down.

Bolan was up with his load and moving toward the Harrier. The draft from the jet's whistling VTOL devices swirled windy turbulence that seemed to draw Bolan and McFee toward the plane by a power of its own.

"It'll be a tight squeeze when we get in," Bolan shouted. "There's only passenger seating for one. Let me get in first. You hunch in low and we'll make it."

"You won't even...know I'm there," McFee promised in gasps.

As Bolan and McFee approached the pulsing body of the jet, Jack Grimaldi emerged from the pilot seat and crouched down on the wing to extend a helping hand to the man Bolan was carrying. Grimaldi's wide grin reminded Bolan more of a kid cutting school to go fishing than an ace pilot making a life-and-death rescue.

"Looks like I got here just in time, Colonel!" he shouted down at Bolan over the engines' roar.

McFee extended his broken hand, which Grimaldi alertly grasped at the wrist. With little effort Grimaldi and Bolan got the injured man up onto the wing of the plane.

"Jack, your timing is so good you ought to be a musician," Bolan called back to the pilot.

Then he turned to meet the faces of Sioung and Tran Le for the last time. The others of the Meo group were nearby, ready to move out. On the lookout for soldiers. But this was a moment that had to be shared.

Sioung was still gripping his shredded, now purple shoulder, yet the Meo leader looked as proud and capable as ever.

"Goodbye, my friend...my brother," he said to Bolan. "Perhaps we meet again."

"Perhaps, Sioung. It can be a small world. Take care."

Then Bolan grabbed Tran Le and left her with one hell of a kiss.

"Goodbye, lady." They hugged each other.

Those sensual lips were close enough to Bolan's slightly injured ear that, despite the smarting pain, he took pleasure in the breath of her full, throaty, lovely voice.

"Goodbye, my strong fighting man. We *will* meet again. I know it in my heart."

There was no more time.

Bolan released the lady from his embrace. He clambered onto the wing of the Harrier, ducked inside and sank into the passenger seat. Grimaldi helped the injured man in gently, then closed the hatch above them. It was a tight fit, yeah. But they made it.

Grimaldi jumped into position up front and goosed the big bird. The high-pitched whistling sound grew louder as the Harrier lifted off.

And in those tumbling moments as the Harrier began its ascent, McFee at last *knew*—when his eyes were again only a few inches from those of the big warrior with whom he shared this tiny space.

"It's you, isn't it, Bolan." McFee did not pronounce it as a question. "I was slow on the uptake back there. But man, no one else fights like that. . . . It *is* you, isn't it, guy?"

"It's me, Colonel. Good to see you again."

"I'd know those iced blues of yours anywhere! I don't know what the Phoenix thing is all about, but goddamn! Thanks for coming back." Then the relief of freedom gave way to a deadly seriousness. "There are a lot of guys just like me who are still in chains in this goddamn stinking hole, Mack."

"Then we'll be coming back."

McFee grunted. "Doesn't that depend on the politicians?"

"That's who sent us this time, pal."

"Guess you're right then. The country got its guts back, did it?"

Bolan's reply was as icy as his eyes. "Maybe. Maybe. We'll see, won't we?"

Bolan looked out and down as the figures of the Meos below him grew smaller. With Deo Roi in the lead and Tran Le at her father's side, the guerrilla band took off at a brisk sprint away from the temple, toward the bank of the Sông Hong.

As the jet lifted off, the Viet army troops behind the pagodas began advancing again on the Monts.

Grimaldi saw this, too, from his pilot seat up front.

"Looks like our friends need some more help," his voice sounded in Bolan's headset.

The VTOL tilted and zapped into another low run over the heads of the pursuing troops.

Again death and hellfire sprouted from the Harrier's underbelly. The regulars saw it coming and were already dispersing when explosions and butchering rounds disrupted their ranks and transformed them into bodies in death spasms and limbs loose from their origins. Those who escaped death scampered back toward the protection of the pagodas or main building.

Trouble appeared in the form of two more MI5 choppers, which were approaching from ten o'clock. But Grimaldi saw them in time and that was that. The VTOL shifted slightly; two more missiles lanced out from its guts; and two more red flowers of flame blossomed in the morning sunlight as Grimaldi's rocket marksmanship scored two direct hits.

Then the ace pilot kicked in the Harrier's afterburners, and they quit that place.

Bolan got one last look through the jet's Plexiglas window at the Meo group below before the VTOL roared him away.

The guerrilla fighters had already made the riverbank. The Meos dropped down the sloping bank and were commencing a dash across the short distance to their waiting sampans.

Yeah, they would make it.

The Hmong were that kind of people. They would always make it. Some way. They would live out the day to fight once more for things that mattered.

A gutsy people.

Guts of the purest sprung steel. Watch out.

EPILOGUE

Grimaldi flew the Harrier out of Vietnamese airspace just as he had jetted her in: barely skimming the tree-tops, zipping along low enough to avoid radar detection, at a speed of 600 mph.

It was 0730 hours.

Jack would not have believed it if he hadn't seen it. In only a matter of hours, the Executioner had dropped into Vietnam and pulled off one impossible mission. And at this moment Grimaldi was ferrying to safety both Bolan and the man of the hour: Colonel Robert McFee, the soldier who knew the whereabouts of numerous American POWs still being held in Vietnam.

And Bolan had accomplished the entire incredible procedure in only four hours. The only trace of the dangers he had overcome was a patch of dried blood on his earlobe.

Hell, the guy had even gotten a goodbye kiss from one of the foxiest little ladies Grimaldi had ever seen in this part of the world.

Yeah, Jack did believe it. He'd been through enough with the bigger-than-life dude to know.

Nothing about Mack Bolan would ever surprise Jack Grimaldi.

He was just damn glad that he'd gotten impatient sitting on his butt back there at that air base in Thailand, waiting for a call-in from Bolan that never came. Impatient enough that he had flown back in anyway. Good thing he had.

At this moment, both of the men who were squeezed into the number-two seat behind Grimaldi were quiet. The pilot didn't blame them. Those would be two worn-out guys back there.

Even for a man like Mack Bolan/John Phoenix, the last four hours had been something else.

It was almost over now. They would be back at the Thai base in no time. Then an airlift to the States.

The mission had been accomplished, yeah.

The Executioner was on his way home.

At least for a while.

There was always the possibility that more action could be accomplished here.

There was always the chance that history might repeat itself.

Had to repeat itself.

That Sergeant Mercy had to once more return to Vietnam.

Always that chance.

OPERATION IMMEDIATE

FR WHITE HOUSE/BROGNOLA 231915Z

TO STONYMAN OPS/PHOENIX

BT

MISSION ALERT X EXERCISE FULL PREROGATIVES X
TOPMAN REQUESTS PHOENIX PERSONAL HANDLING X
DAUGHTER OF TOP US HI-TECH CONTRACTOR
HARRISON BRETON KIDNAPPED THIS AM IN ALGIERS
X TYPICAL TERRORIST DAYLIGHT STRIKE ON
PUBLIC STREET X BRETON'S FIRM DEVELOPING
ULTRA SECRET LOW YIELD NUCLEAR DEVICE
CODENAMED LITTLE BANG CAPABLE OF
CONCEALMENT IN STANDARD ATTACHE CASE X
BRETON HIMSELF DISAPPEARED SHORTLY AFTER
NEWSBREAK X LITTLE BANG PROTOTYPE ALSO
MISSING X IMPLICATIONS OBVIOUS X INTERCEPT
BRETON AND RECOVER PROTOTYPE AT ANY COST
REPEAT AT ANY COST X DATA PACKAGE IN COMPUTER
FILE ZEBRA X EXERCISE OWN DISCRETION RE
KIDNAPPEE ONCE NATIONAL SECURITY
IMPERATIVES ACHIEVED X ACKNOWLEDGE AND
CONFIRM SOONEST

BT

231915Z EOM

OPERATIONAL URGENT
FR STONYMAN 231955Z
TO BROGNOLA/WH/WASHDC
BT
APRIL SENDS RE LITTLE BANG X PHOENIX LAUNCHED
X ALL STONYMAN FORCES ALERTED FOR STANDBY
CONTINGENCIES X SUGGEST DESIGNATE STONYMAN
OPS MISSION CENTRAL FOR ALL COMM DATA INTEL
AND ALL OTHER MISSION REQUIREMENTS X CLEAR
COMSAT LINK ALL USEMB IN TARGET REGION X CLEAR
NAVCOMM LINK NSS WASHDC COMSIXTHFLT FOR
MISSION SUPPORT REQUIREMENTS
BT
231955Z EOM

MACK BOLAN

THE EXECUTIONER 44

appears again in
Terrorist Summit
by DON PENDLETON

**Coming in August
from Gold Eagle Books**

MACK BOLAN
THE EXECUTIONER 44

Terrorist Summit

It was in Vietnam that Sergeant Mack Samuel Bolan first earned the title The Executioner, tallying 97 verified kills of high-ranking Viet-Cong officers and Communist officials. His return to Vietnam in search of an important POW has marked the completion of a crucial cycle in his life.

But there are other returns, circles within circles. In TERRORIST SUMMIT, Mack Bolan finds himself back in North Africa. He tackles an evil international Mafia of terrorism by the azure bays of Algeria, where a hostage drama unfolds that is so merciless it could cripple the U.S.

The Executioner had visited North Africa before. It seemed a lifetime ago.... He had just finished bearding the Mafia lion in its own den. Those foreigners had proved no better able to withstand the "Bolan effect" than their American cousins. But Bolan had been seriously wounded in the fray, barely escaping across the Mediterranean to the North A... can coast, to recuperate and regroup.

Now Bolan was back. This time the action concerned a neat little piece of nuclear blackmail. The secret to defusing the scheme was a woman, hardly more than a girl. Unless Mack Bolan found her within twenty-four hours, it would mean a terrorist victory of a magnitude that could undo all that Bolan had accomplished thus far in his New War.

The scale of the danger was monstrously big. . . but the action was still deadly personal:

Bolan and Tex pulled the jeep up to the gate and leaned on the horn. They were here to root out Luke Harker, at this moment the single most dangerous person in the world.

The guard pinched the cigarette butt from between his lips, flicked it off to one side, and took his time about coming out of the little guardhouse.

"I thought you was in Algiers," he said to Tex Hoffman, not bothering to look at Bolan.

"Harker," Bolan demanded. His voice was low and even, nearly a monotone, except for something cold and dark that forced the guard to look at him.

Bolan was dressed in light cotton-twill slacks, a gold shirt with a designer's symbol prominent on the breast pocket, expensive rubber-soled deck shoes, and shades in gold aviator frames.

e took a folded piece of paper from the dash, held it up and repeated, "Harker."

The armed guard smiled in a twisted, sardonic way. He was going to teach this dude a few things, and he was going to enjoy giving the lesson.

"Who is this clown, Tex?" he said, and reached for the paper.

What happened then was too fast for the gunman to follow. All he knew was that suddenly he was bent forward over the hood of the jeep, the hot metal scorching his cheek. The "clown," still seated behind the windshield, had reached and bent back the tough boy's arm toward his neck. The maneuver sent stabbing pains through his shoulder.

"Harker," Bolan said a third time, in that same emotionless voice.

It was almost like the slob was on a run of stupidity that he didn't want to break. He started to claw clumsily at the Makarov automatic at his hip with his free hand.

Bolan wrenched up on the arm he was holding. It snapped just below the elbow like a turkey's wishbone. The jagged end of the small bone of the forearm tore through the skin, glistening whitely as blood welled up around it.

The guard let out a high mewling squeal. Bolan released him. He slumped to the rock-strewn ground and lay there moaning. Bolan

pulled himself out of his seat and struck the gu
behind the ear with the guy's own pistol. Tha
stopped the moaning.

"Let's move," said Bolan. He was as ready as
he would ever be to confront the man who was
holding the world for ransom.

Watch for *Terrorist Summit*, Executioner #44, wherever paperback books are sold—August, 1982.